ATHENA V. LORD

THE LUCK OF
Z.A.P. AND ZOE

ILLUSTRATED BY
JEAN JENKINS

MACMILLAN PUBLISHING COMPANY
New York
COLLIER MACMILLAN PUBLISHERS
London

Macmillan Publishing Company
866 Third Avenue, New York, NY 10022
Collier Macmillan Canada, Inc.
First Edition
Printed in the United States of America

10   9   8   7   6   5   4   3   2   1

The text of this book is set in 12 point Century Schoolbook.
The illustrations are rendered in pencil.

Library of Congress Cataloging-in-Publication Data
Lord, Athena V.
The luck of Z.A.P. and Zoe.
Summary: The continuing adventures of eleven-year-old
Zach and his little sister Zoe living in a small city in
upstate New York in 1940.
[1. Greek-Americans—Fiction. 2. Brothers and
sisters—Fiction] I. Loewer, Jean Jenkins, ill.
II. Title. III. Title: Luck of ZAP and Zoe.
PZ7.L8769Lu   1987   [Fic]   87-5545
ISBN 0-02-759560-9

To Edith and Hershel Samuels,
old and dear friends,
with appreciation for their contribution
to the writing of this book

Contents

1 The Yankee Team 1

2 The Business of Secrets 25

3 The New-Style Holiday 53

4 The Might of Right 79

5 The Big Move 104

6 All for One 129

1

The Yankee Team

Everybody oughtta have an ambition. It gives a person something to look forward to. Like Christmas, if you know what I mean. Mine for this summer is to grow up. Don't mistake me. My brain is plenty big enough, bigger than most people's. It's muscles that I'm short on.

Because my initials spell ZAP, I have the kids on our block of Mohawk Street almost believing that, like Captain Marvel, I can call up secret powers by saying that special word. All I need now is some muscles to convince them for sure.

I'd worked out a plan for building up my muscles by doing push-ups and chin-ups twice a day, every day. But today I couldn't seem to get started. Thinking about the whole summer that lay ahead was discouraging me.

We own the Miss Liberty Lunch in Cohoes, a city in upstate New York not far from Albany, the capital. Owning the Miss Liberty means that Papa and Mama both are tied up working in the store all day long. Summers when school's out, I have the job of keeping an eye on my peanut-sized sister, Zoe. Anybody who thinks that's not work, doesn't know Zoe. Taking care of her for the four summers she's been on earth proves I'm not afraid of hard work. But I'd much rather do *real* work, the kind that pays money.

I help out in the store, too, so I don't have much free time for pay jobs. And no pay means I can't buy any fireworks for the Fourth of July.

I had just come to this sad conclusion when Ferdie Gaudet, who's a month older than me—he's already twelve—came down the street. Ferdie stopped at our stoop, where I was sitting on the bottom step.

Waving a brown paper bag under my nose, he said in a gloating kind of voice, "Hey, Zach Poulos, thanks to Tante Marie, I just got a penny's worth of punk and a penny's worth of snakes. My shoebox is practically full and we got almost a week to go still."

That's the trouble with our family. Being Greek and like newcomers to the U.S.A., all our relatives are thousands and thousands of miles away over the ocean in Greece. No great-aunts like Tante Marie here to give us a penny now and then, no grandmas to visit or look after Zoe. That can make a big difference in a kid's life, as anybody can see by looking at Ferdie and me.

"You don't have any yet, do you? You can watch me shoot mine," Ferdie offered, as if he was doing me a real favor.

"Are you absolutely, positively *sure* I can watch, Ferdie?" I asked.

"Listen, after I put my stuff away, let's get some of the guys and play Knights on Horseback in the backyard."

Gaudets live next door, in an upstairs flat like us. Just an alley separates our two buildings, and we share a big backyard with them and some other houses.

Though Knights is a game that I, myself, made up, I shuddered. The last time we played was a Monday, washday. Ducking in and out of the bottoms of the clean, wet sheets, we ended up pulling them off the clotheslines in the backyard. When Mama spotted those sheets lying in the dirt, I expected to see steam come out of the top of her head like a volcano. Even now, the memory of what happened after makes me feel queasy.

"Uh-uh! I can't believe you'd bring it up on a day like today. Ferdie, you must have a lump of fat where everybody else has brains," I answered.

His snappy comeback to that was "Aw, you're just jealous 'cause I'm going to have the best Fourth of anybody."

"Imm-possible!" I told him. "Human beings by nature can't be jealous of jackasses."

3

But to tell the honest-to-God truth, I *was* kinda depressed. I could see no way to make any money before the holiday. For days, weeks, every kid in town had been scrounging empties from alleys, yards and even off people's back porches. There couldn't be an unclaimed soda bottle left in the city of Cohoes. Most likely, I'd have to talk Ferdie into sharing his shoebox.

That wouldn't be too hard. I can usually talk Ferdie and most of the kids into doing what I want. But still, not having my own pile got me. After all, this Fourth is the last, the very last chance for us kids to shoot off our own fireworks. Thanks to our do-goody governor, it's gonna be against the law to sell, buy or shoot off fireworks in the state of New York after this August 1, 1940.

"Anyway, I have to go in. Since Zoe's not playing with your sister, Monique, I'd better check on her," I told Ferdie.

Sometimes Zoe comes in handy as an excuse. What I really intended was to go get some new library books. Ferdie doesn't understand why I'm always going to the library, but it's free and I like to read. A good book right now would take my mind off my empty pockets.

At the library I had three books ready to check out, but Miss Rollins, the librarian, and the skinny lady ahead of me just kept on talking in those whispery voices that people use in libraries.

4

" . . . so there's nobody to take care of him, and I can't take him with me to my mother-in-law's camp. She's allergic, you see," said the skinny lady.

"My dear, I suffer from the same condition. That's why I can't help you," Miss Rollins answered.

I was suffering, too, mostly from impatience. Zoe had agreed to wait at home for me instead of tagging along only because I had promised to bring her a new book to read. If I stayed away much longer, she was bound to complain to Mama.

"It wrecks any chance of our getting away for a long weekend over the Fourth. John will be so disappointed," the skinny lady added in a gloomy whisper. "I'm so upset. I wish I could just chain him. He's so young and active that . . . ."

Chain *him*? She couldn't mean to chain the John that she had said would be so disappointed? I gave my books a shove across the loan desk to remind the ladies that they were not alone in the library.

Picking up her three books finally, the lady sighed and said, "I'd give anything . . . everything to find someone to take care of him for a couple of hours a day."

The last dozen words settled in my mind like a pigeon come to roost. Wasn't that what I'd been doing all these years? Only not a him, I take care of a her. But wa-it a minute. This lady was willing

5

to give anything. A person who was willing to give anything should be willing to give money, right?

"Lady, I'm *it*!" I whooped out loud.

"*SSSshush*," said Miss Rollins in disapproval.

Lowering my voice to a whisper, I said, "I mean, lady, I'll take care of him. My name is Zachary A. Poulos and I'd be happy to take the job."

As she looked me over from head to toe, the lady said doubtfully, "You're not very big. I don't know if you can handle . . . ."

This was too important to be polite. I interrupted her. "That's right. You don't know. But you should see what I've been handling every summer. And I can take on another one, too."

Suddenly remembering what Papa says about business, I added, "A satisfied customer always comes back. Every summer, they ask me to do this job again, so you know I must be doing good work."

Mainly, I tell the truth. I just didn't think it absolutely necessary to add that Papa and Mama had nobody else to do the job!

"How much do you know about taking care of . . . ."

I cut in quickly. "I know all about it, lady. I told you I'm experienced. And you wouldn't have to pay me a lot and I'm strong and . . . ."

The lady burst out laughing. I think it was the sight of the muscle that I made to show her how strong I was, but I didn't care. The important thing

6

was to convince her to give me the job.

Miss Rollins said, "He *does* return his library books on time, Mrs. Cusack."

I couldn't see what that had to do with the job, but I followed it up by saying, "I read aloud real well, too. I bet he'd like that."

For some reason Mrs. Cusack laughed out loud again. She nodded to the librarian and said, "You're right. Half the problem is being able to depend on someone." She turned to me. "Come home with me now and we'll see if he likes you. Then we can settle the pay and I'll show you what needs doing."

Even though it might kill my chance to get the job, I said, "I gotta go home first and tell my . . . my family where I'm going." I had crossed my fingers because actually I had to go home mostly to get Zoe occupied.

But Mrs. Cusack seemed to approve of me more than ever and gave me her address, way down on Mohawk Street. We agreed to meet there at two. I was on air walking home. If the job lasted four or five days, I might even make a whole quarter.

When I told Mama, she beamed and said, "That was clever of you, Zachary, to see the opportunity."

"Isn't opportunity what America is all about? Exactly," said Papa, answering his own question. "And here you help the lady while helping yourself. Don't forget, though: You must do the noon dishwashing and all your other work here as usual."

"No problem, Papa. All it takes is a couple of hours a day, the lady told me. And I'm sure I can pick when to do it."

"Then pick a time, Zach, when I can go, too. I wanna see who you're going to take care of. Maybe we can be friends and I'll play with him," Zoe said, wiggling on her chair in excitement.

"Uh-uh!" I said. I was *not* going to show up for this job with a baby sister tagging after me. "You heard Papa, Zoe. Store duties first," I reminded her.

Since she started kindergarten, Zoe's very touchy about being treated like a baby. When school let out in June, she complained about not having any "work" to do. Mama agreed that a girl going into first grade was a big girl, and she gave Zoe a regular job.

Every day after the noon rush hour, Zoe carries out a little pan of soapy water and washes the oilcloth covers of the tables in our lunchroom with a rag. Then she gets clean rinse water and does them again. She has to stand on a chair to reach, and the job takes her a long time, I'm happy to say.

I hit the bell at the side door of Mrs. Cusack's house just as the two o'clock freight train blew its whistle at the crossing. The doorbell had only the one name by it. She must be rich to have a whole house all to herself, I thought, and the big backyard with a high wire fence all around proved it. Now if only the little kid wasn't spoiled.

"Over here, Zachary. Come in and I'll introduce you to my baby," said Mrs. Cusack, waving at me from the gate in the fence. She let me in through the gate, but instead of going into the house, she headed toward the back of the yard, calling "Come" as she walked.

Whoosh!

Looking to the right and behind me, I couldn't see anything to account for the rush of air that I had felt on the back of my legs. But I heard Mrs. Cusack saying between laughs, "Yes, yes, I see you."

Looking ahead again, I felt my eyes pop wide and I gulped as I saw the "baby" who now stood at her side. Some baby!

"A new friend, Yankee. This is Zachary Poulos, Zach to you, my baby," she said, stroking his head.

Big and solid looking, Yankee was an all black dog with a broad chest and a powerful jaw. He quivered as if he couldn't wait to leap into the air. No wonder Mrs. Cusack laughed when I said I'd read aloud to him!

"What . . . what is he?"

"I thought you knew all about dogs," said Mrs. Cusack. She sounded suspicious.

"I didn't thi . . . I mean, I do, but mostly the neighborhood ones aren't . . . I mean, he's special, isn't he?" Mostly the neighborhood ones are scrawny mutts, and they don't have an air of being ready to run you to a shadow.

"He certainly is. He's a purebred black Labrador retriever, and the best field dog in Albany County. I have a blue ribbon to prove it."

Lucky for me, dog owners are just like mamas of human babies. Mrs. Cusack got so busy telling me about Yankee's family and how truly special he was, she forgot completely her suspicions of how much I knew about dogs. Then she took me around, showing me the leash and the dry dog food in the shed and where the outdoor water faucet was.

"Change his water every day, and don't forget: He needs good, hard exercise twice a day," said Mrs. Cusack.

She put me to work right away, making me practice putting on his leash and giving him the commands to "Sit" and "Come." Yankee and I went for a short walk around the block to get acquainted, and it was a pleasure, believe you me. That Yankee listened to me a lot better than Zoe ever does. Another plus I discovered was that my muscles got a real workout hanging on to that leash.

Mrs. Cusack looked happy as she took Yankee from me. Putting the key to the gate and a coin in my hand, she said, "You get half your pay now and the other half when we come back from our holiday."

Twenty-five cents and that was only *half* my pay! I felt richer than King Croesus with all his gold. I couldn't wait to spend it, and I didn't. Detouring to La Marche's on Remsen Street, I took my pick of the fireworks.

The sight of three cigar boxes full to overflowing with tiny squibs, regular firecrackers, cannon crackers and caps for my cap pistol made Ferdie's jaw drop open so far that a horse could have walked in. I had, besides, pinwheels, four Roman candles and some sparklers and snakes for Zoe.

"What a haul! You must have robbed a bank," he said finally, after closing his jaw with a snap. "What time are you going to shoot yours off? Will you tell me so I can watch?"

Watching Ferdie lick his lips hungrily, I got an inspiration.

"You know what, Ferdie? This last Fourth for us kids oughtta be such a bang-up one that nobody will ever forget it to their dying days. Let's all pool our stuff and shoot off everything together."

Sometimes Ferdie's nose gets out of joint when I have ideas, but this one suited him to a T. We spread the word that night after supper. With four days to go and kids still buying, there was no telling how many pieces we would end up with in the

11

stockpile. Having put in a lion's share to start, I could rest easy and dream about how I was going to spend the second half of my pay after the Fourth.

Well, I didn't exactly rest, since I had both my chores and my new job to take care of. After washing up the breakfast dishes, I raced to get Yankee for his morning exercise. I felt a little nervous about being on my own with him and wondered if he'd remember me. But I didn't need to worry. Yankee acted like we'd been friends from the year One.

When I took him into the lunchroom—on the leash, of course—Papa told me that I had to go with Mama to take Zoe to her doctor's appointment. Mama's English isn't so good yet, and she wanted me there just in case.

"That's a good dog, looks strong and quick," said Papa. He came out from behind the counter to admire Yankee and scratch in back of his ears. "When I was a boy in the Old Country taking care of the sheep, we had . . . ."

I never found out what Papa had been going to tell me about dogs in Greece. Yankee, who had spotted Zoe running into the store at full speed, bounded up to greet her. Zoe tried to brake, but it was no use. The two connected like a bat with a ball, and the *thwack* as Zoe bounced off Yankee was so loud I'll bet you could hear it clear across the street.

"*Eeyah!*" She ended in a heap on the floor. A second look at Yankee with his powerful chest and jaw sent her head down into her knees. Arms wrapped around her head, she began to cry and screech at the same time. "Goway . . . goway. . . ."

"Zoe, Zoe, stop. You'll make yourself sick with all that crying. It's a nice doggie. Stop, *Zoeitsa*." Papa picked her up to calm her, but as soon as he peeled her arms down, she wrapped them back around her head.

She was . . . what's the word? Hysterical. There was no speaking to her, no calming her. Papa jerked his head at me to get the dog out of the store, and I went out to sit on the bottom step, shaking my head. How could we go to the doctor's with Zoe sobbing every inch of the way?

Papa said pretty much the same thing when he came out. He added, "You'll have to remove him from here. Take him back. Maybe you should give up the job?"

"I *can't,* Papa. Mrs. Cusack is counting on me and she's already gone. Besides, I've spent the money." I answered through lips that felt numb.

"Zachary, you are sometimes too quick, my boy. You took this without thinking through. Now you must think to find a way, a way that permits you to do the job without scaring Zoe and without neglecting her."

Papa was right. I had talked myself into this.

But how could such a good idea add up so wrong?

Since Mama always fusses about having clean underwear and dressing up for a visit to the doctor, I had time before she needed me to translate. Papa agreed that I could meet Mama and Zoe at the doctor's rather than walk there with them.

Before returning Yankee home, I took him—running all the way—down to the flats behind Root's Mill. The way Yankee leaned into me, touching his shoulder to my leg, he must have thought we were two dog friends running together.

Thinking through, the way Papa said to do, didn't produce any brilliant solutions. If I didn't take Yankee out every day for exercise, he'd howl and the neighbors would tell Mrs. Cusack. If I did take him out, I'd have to bring him down into our neighborhood so that I could keep an eye on Zoe, too, and *she* would yowl. My brain got dizzy from chasing the problem around in circles.

By the time I'd thrown a big stick half a dozen times for Yankee to retrieve, I'd stopped grinding my teeth. It was purely joy and pleasure to watch him race and be under that stick, waiting, before it even started down. That dog would have made a terrific outfielder for the Brooklyn Dodgers.

"*Woo-eee.*"

I heard a whistle of admiration and turned to see Ferdie and Karl Schmidt coming through the tall grass toward me.

"Isn't that a black Labrador?" asked Karl. "I saw a Lab once jump and catch a duck in midair out at the Rod and Gun Club Fall Shoot. Maybe it was him."

They both looked respectfully at Yankee, who wagged his tail, and then at me. Seeing that same respectful look carried over to me stirred up a germ of an idea. Did I say that I'm a speedy thinker as well as a speedy talker? A game plan came to me on the spot.

"Yessirree, I'm glad I talked Mrs. Cusack into letting me help *train* her *champion* Lab. That's something not too many kids our age get a chance at."

"Trainer, nothing," Ferdie scoffed. "You're just playing with him."

I gave this very confident, knowing chuckle.

"Ferdie, your stupidity is matched only by your ignorance. Why d'ya think I got so much money? Yankee is a black Labrador *retriever*. What d'ya think he's judged on besides his looks?" I waited a second to let that sink in and then added, "Of course, experience like this really pays off once you're grown up and can take on a lotta dogs."

Ferdie's big Adam's apple bounced up and down as he swallowed hard. Thinking always gets Ferdie excited. He shifted to get a better look at Yankee.

"Say, Zach, you haven't forgotten our club rules?

Share and share alike." Ferdie added, "I don't mean the money, but you should give us a turn training Yankee."

Good old Ferdie! Eyeing Ferdie's long ape arms, I figured he'd have no trouble hanging on to Yankee. Still, I made my voice sound doubtful as I said, "He's a very valuable dog. I don't know if—"

Karl interrupted me. "We'll settle, the both of us, for taking one turn together. You can count on me to be careful, Zach. You know that."

True enough. Karl's the kind who not only checks but double-checks every instruction before gluing even one little piece on his model airplanes.

I let myself be convinced. While I was at the doctor's, Ferdie and Karl both acquired some of the valuable experience that I'd mentioned: They exercised Yankee. Naturally, I took charge of getting him back to his yard.

After supper that evening, I tried to hustle through my chore of getting Zoe ready for bed, but it took forever to get her in the house, washed and under the covers. By the time I went to take Yankee for his second exercise period, it was good and dark.

On the way home, I made up my mind never to go that late again. The dark doesn't scare me, but it sure made it hard to see Yankee and to find the leash. To top it all off, the next-door neighbor thought I was stealing the dog and came out yelling.

Mama let me put Papa's gold watch on my nightstand so I could get up at five-thirty the next morning. Stretching my days out at either end was not my idea of a good time, but I had Yankee fed and exercised before Zoe cracked even one eye open. I arrived back on our doorstep just as Papa unlocked the store door.

Papa, who looked as tired as I felt, said, "You been finding ways to do your job, *Zaharia*? I do believe you're more stubborn than Zoe, even. This is good for getting work done."

Maybe so. Seven more exercise periods still to go, I reminded myself. But in the meantime, I had Ferdie and Karl nicely set up to lighten my load.

"In the meantime" didn't last one half day. That afternoon Karl had to weed vegetables on his aunt's farm and Ferdie went fishing with his uncle up to Saratoga Lake. Once again I had only myself to count on. I plunked Zoe in the library with a pile of books while I raced to take care of Yankee. Superman flying through the sky couldn't have moved any faster than I did.

Greeting me back at the library, Zoe's whispers grew louder and louder. "I wanna go home, Zach. The libarian don't like me laughing out loud and I'm tired of sitting straight in the chair and . . . ."

"Sss-sh." I could see Miss Rollins frowning at us, and I still needed to get new books.

Being around books seems to make my brain cells work better. My problem had two parts, I decided. First, Zoe hasn't known very many animals having four legs, one on each corner, and an *unknown* makes for the scariest kind of fear, *I* think. Yankee was unknown and big. Which is the second part of the problem: Zoe's size. She's so small that her view of the world must be different from the rest of us. For instance, when we play, nobody ever picks her for any team or side.

On the library shelves, I spotted a solution to the first part of the problem. Putting Zoe's choice back, I slipped a big green book into our pile. She never noticed until we sat on the bottom step of the stoop to read again.

"Hey, I didn't pick this. Take it back, Zach," she ordered.

"Wait. Let's look at the pictures first, anyway." Leaning over, I turned pages to find the colored illustrations.

"Oh-hh. They're cute. Whadda ya call those, Zach?"

"Scotch terriers. Scotties, they call them. Hey, look at that police dog."

"Does he belong to the police? Why's he called that? Read me what it says, Zach," she commanded.

I let my breath out in relief. Zoe's curiosity was caught but good. She can read for herself, but when she really really wants to know something, she gets too impatient to do it.

"Well, it says police dogs were taught 'to tackle crooks in such fashion as to trip up and subdue them. . . .'" I read on through *The Dog Book* by Albert Payson Terhune about cocker spaniels, Boston bulldogs, Alaskan huskies, every kind of dog you can imagine, and it's unbelievable what some of them can do. It read better than a fairy tale. I almost forgot to make my next move.

Standing up, I said, "Uh, speaking of dogs, I'm going to exer . . . to . . . uh . . . put Yankee through his tricks."

Zoe frowned and bit her bottom lip. Making up her mind suddenly, she asked, "Will . . . will he be loose? Or c'n you keep him on that rope thing? I wanna watch him do his tricks."

"Heck, Zoe, there's a big fence. You can stand by it. Remember, Yankee doesn't know you, so don't try to boss him around, and don't upset him by crying. Don't make him sad," I warned.

"Don't you 'don't' me, Zachary Athanasius Poulos," Zoe said indignantly. "Everybody—Stanley, the policeman, Georgie's cat—everybody likes me."

The idea that *she* might upset the dog instead of vice-versa occupied Zoe all the way to Mrs.

Cusack's, just as I'd planned. With the fence between them, Zoe flinched only a little when Yankee ran by her, chasing the sticks that I threw. She couldn't get over how he never missed. My arm was practically dropping off by the time I thought it okay to quit.

I had softened Zoe up considerably, but still, I needed to be able to take Yankee *out* of the yard for his exercise. On the way back from the next A.M. run, I worked out the finishing touches to my plan. Wording it just right would be tricky but not any harder than getting up at five-thirty, I figured.

"Zoe, where's your flag, the little one we bought at the Fourth of July parade last year?" I asked, shaking her awake.

"You can't have it. I'm gonna carry it when we go watch the big parade. Whadda ya want it for?"

Zoe's curiosity bump is almost as big as mine. I knew I had been right to count on it. I crossed my fingers that the next part would work just as well.

"Oh, I don't want it in the morning. I need it for *our* parade just before supper on the Fourth."

"Our parade? What's that? We all going to march where?" She sat bolt upright now, black eyes wide open.

"Remember? Everybody's going to shoot fireworks together. But first we'll parade around the block and up Remsen Street so people will know and come to watch. C'mon, give me the flag 'cause

20

there's hardly enough time left to train Yankee."

"Train Yankee? To do what?"

"No time, I tell you, to talk about it. I gotta find Monique Gaudet and get her started."

"What's Monique got to do in this? It's our flag and our dog. Why's she gonna do anything?"

When I heard the "our dog," I let my fingers uncross. "It's like a show and we're going to have George Washington coming with his horse at the head of his soldiers. On accounta it's a small size flag, the person carrying it has to be small or it'll look funny."

Zoe, who had been scrambling into her clothes, straightened up and stuck out her pointed chin. Her eyes narrowed and she reached up to jab me in the chest with her finger. "*I'm* smaller than Monique, and besides, her hair's too long and she's not your sister. I am."

"Yeah, you'd be perfect. But . . . well, whoever plays George will carry the flag and lead Yankee like he was a horse, maybe even ride on his back. I think you should just watch from the corner," I suggested.

"You better take another think, Zachary Athanasius Poulos. Anything you think that dumb Monique can do, I can do and better. You want my flag, you have to take me, too. And you know, when I make up my mind, it stays made up," Zoe warned.

"I've noticed!" Then I said slowly, like someone

giving in, "We-ll, if you're sure you won't screech like an idiot. And if you promise not to go all mushy over him. Y'know how you hate it when visiting ladies slobber all over you."

That last bit, giving the two of them the same dislikes, was a neat touch. Zoe nodded so hard in agreement that her thick black hair bounced up like an umbrella popping open.

Not to brag or anything, but I trained her in just two days' time. Papa, who reads us the Greek myths sometimes, says that not even Hercules, the strong man, could have done the job any faster or better.

From standing a foot away and touching Yankee timidly with one fingertip, Zoe worked up to walking at his side with an arm slung over his shoulder. It made for a great picture, because in our parade Zoe wore the general's hat that I'd made of paper and Yankee's tongue stuck out as if he was laughing.

She kept her promise, too. Although the reporter and the photographer from the *Cohoes American* tried to coax her into different poses, she wouldn't hug or kiss Yankee.

Did I say that the picture of us kids and the story headlined COHOES YANKEES CELEBRATE made the front page? Some customers brought us extra copies, but I don't need any newspaper article to remember this Fourth. Every time I catch even a whiff of a burnt match, I see in my head

eight of us twirling three sparklers in each hand. I mean, sixty-four sparklers looping in the dark is not going to be forgotten soon; neither are two dozen Roman candles skyrocketing in the air at the same time.

Of course, they couldn't get the fireworks in a still picture, but that reporter didn't tell the half of it. He didn't tell about Papa bringing out all the chairs from the restaurant for Ferdie's Tante and the other old people, so that we ended up with a real sit-down audience for our fireworks show. Or about Mr. O'Heaney treating every kid who was under twelve to an ice-cream cone.

And he never told about Mr. Schmidt and Mrs. Gaudet waltzing together in the street to the tunes Mr. Luddy played on his harmonica. The grownups said it was champion ballroom-style dancing, but I thought it looked like an elephant dancing with a flea.

I oughtta be satisfied, I guess, 'cause it's something for a kid my age to have his name in the paper. Still, I wish the photographer had been more careful when he took the picture. Oh, you can see plain enough that it's Karl with the wooden sword who's saluting the flag, and Ferdie playing a tattoo on the drum. And of course, nobody can mistake the Luddy twins who're blowing horns. Me? I'm the face you can't see, the one hidden by the flag Zoe's carrying.

2

The Business of
Secrets

I used to like secrets—making them, keeping them—but that was before last night.

"Hurry up, Zach. It's your move," Ferdie urged me.

Ferdie's voice cut into my gloomy thoughts as he shoved the dice across the board. Whenever someone tries to hustle you into throwing the dice, watch out. It usually means he's landed on your property and is trying to skip paying rent. I looked over the board, and sure enough, Ferdie's piece was sitting on the Water Works, which I owned.

"Fork over the rent first, Ferdie."

"I'll have to mortgage something to pay you. Lemme owe it to you," Ferdie begged.

Making up my mind suddenly, I said, "Time out. I don't wanna play anymore."

Since I was winning, Ferdie looked confused. It's a fact of life that nobody quits while he's ahead. But after what I'd heard last night, I needed time to myself.

"Leave the board set up for another day. I'll keep Zoe out of here," I added. I might not feel like playing now, but I didn't intend to lose my advantage.

Our game was set up in the Bonelli Electric Supply Company store, which is right next door to us on Mohawk Street. Actually, the two places are connected by an inside door from our kitchen because the Electric Company part has no water; next door has to use our toilet and sink.

It's been empty since January. One day Bonelli was there, and the next, he wasn't. A lot of stuff just got left behind: the desk stuffed with unpaid bills, a kind of greasy workbench, crates with bits of old wire. No tools, but a whole roll and a half of black friction tape. We put a good grip on Georgie La Rouche's bat by wrapping some of that tape around the bottom, and the rest we wrapped around a little red ball to make a new softball. Today, looking at Bonelli's junk gave me the creeps. I shivered.

"You're coming down with something," Ferdie said suspiciously. "Is it catching?"

"No . . . yes . . . I mean, I don't know. You better beat it, Ferdie. See ya later," I answered, leading him to the front door of Number 26 and sliding the bolt back to let him out.

That's *if* I'm here, I'll see you, I added to myself as I closed the door behind him. We might have to get out as fast as Bonelli did after he got the letter from the bank.

If only I hadn't gotten up to go to the bathroom in the middle of the night, I could be ignorant and happy like Zoe. On my way back to bed, I was trying to work out why water always swirls clockwise as it drains out of the toilet. That's when a sharp "No" from Papa and Mama's room stopped me dead in my tracks. All our doors are open in the summer to catch the breeze, so you could hardly say I was listening in on somebody's private conversation.

"No," Papa repeated. "You already work too many hours here in the house and the store. You can't go."

Go? Where did Mama want to go?

By the time I climbed back into bed, I had heard the answer to my question and more.

No wonder Papa has been looking so tired. Leaving Mama to close up the Miss Liberty, he's been working nights as chef at the Capitol Restaurant down the street. This week the Capitol's regular chef, who'd been sick, came back, so Papa's finished working there. The trouble is we *need* the nine dollars he's been earning each week. Mama wanted to pick up extra cash by sorting rags at one of the factories on the hill. And that's when Papa said no.

Still thinking hard, I got a glass of milk from

the icebox and sat down at the kitchen table. I felt like somebody with brain rot because I couldn't really understand what I'd heard last night. To sum it up: *We have no money.*

What I didn't understand was how come we have no money when customers are in the store all day long and the cash register keeps ringing.

I couldn't ask Mama and Papa about it; their whispering in the night meant they didn't want Zoe and me to know. Anyway, they would probably lie. Grownups think it's all right to do that to kids when it's "for their own good."

"Zach, get me some milk, too," said Zoe, barging into the kitchen and into my thoughts. "I want chocolate, though."

"You'll take white and like it," I told Zoe, pouring her a small glass. "Chocolate costs more money."

"I don't drink white. You know that," Zoe complained. "Give me my regular chocolate."

Zoe hates milk. She hates milk so much that Papa had to order a strawberry-flavored milk specially for her to build her up after she'd been sick.

"You can't have it. Grow up, kid, and drink white."

"I won't. I won't 'n' you can't make me. I'm gonna tell on you. You'll be sor-ree," Zoe said.

"The dairy charges us more for chocolate and strawberry, and we can't afford it. *We have no money, Zoe.* D'you hear me?"

"We can *all* hear you, *Zaharia.*" Papa spoke to me in Greek, as he came into the kitchen. He does that when he doesn't want the customers out front to understand. "You know already, Zach, that it's bad to beat an animal with a stick to make it obey. You *should* know, too, that it's equally bad to beat or bully your little sister with words," he continued.

"Even if I'm sweet as pie to Zoe, it doesn't change anything. We still won't have any money, and the bank is still going to put us out on the street for not paying the rent."

There. I'd said the words out loud. It was a relief, even though Papa might call me a fresh kid who talked back.

"Shouting at Zoe is going to bring us more money, do you think?" Papa asked in a mild voice that surprised me. He added, "I take it you were awake in the night?"

"I had to go to the bathroom," I said defensively. "I'm only trying to help. At least we oughtta save the cash profit that we haven't got."

That last sentence didn't sound quite right to me, but I didn't want to stop and sort it out. I had an important favor to ask him.

"I can help. I'm old enough. The only thing is: Can we leave after dark when the guys aren't around?"

"Whoa, boy," Papa said. "We're not going to be out on the street tonight or tomorrow, I promise you. You're right about one thing, though: You are old enough to know our family's affairs."

The way Papa told it, there was nothing deep or hard to understand. We *had* money but it wasn't exactly in our hands. That is, we had earned money by giving meals to customers, but we were still waiting to be paid by the city.

The men on the public works—fixing streets and sewers and such—get vouchers or tickets for a lunch in any lunchroom or restaurant that's agreed to cooperate. Since customers get more for the money at our place, most of them come to us. We punch the tickets for the amounts they eat, and then the city adds it all up and gives us the cash. Only the city was way behind in paying its bills because it gets the money from Washington. In June we'd been paid for the January and February meals.

"What cash money we get from other customers, Zachary, goes to buy our supplies—the milk, the eggs, the bread, the ice—and there is not enough after that for the rent. The bank's policy is to evict when three months are owed, and that's what we're coming up to now." Papa paused, his face sober. "I am going to explain to the bank president himself that we have not yet got our money. I hope, I think . . . he will surely wait, even as we must.

For now, you are not to worry your head or Zoe's," he ordered.

Under the table Zoe gave me a kick in the shins that made me wince.

"So there, Zachary Athanasius Poulos. Give me my chocolate milk. Or I won't grow, and you'll have to take care of me all my life."

The expression on my face must have been something to see because Papa gave a bark of laughter. Pouring Zoe's milk, I gave her a look that promised to get even for both the kick and the smart-aleck remark.

For the next minute, we were all quiet. I made up my mind. If I was old enough to be told, I was old enough to contribute.

Swallowing hard, I said, "I have a quarter still. Take it, please, Papa, to help with the rent."

"Thank you, Zachary, but we need forty-eight dollars more to catch up, and I don't like to take your . . . ." Then, clapping me on the back like he does with his men friends, Papa said, "Meantime, Zach, if you find any gold in the streets, let me know."

That's an old joke among Greeks. When a newcomer from the Old Country shows up, they give him directions for finding the street in America that's paved with gold. Don't I wish it was true, though.

Papa had said not to worry, but all day long, I

31

seesawed between wondering if the bank would wait for its rent and hunting for ways to get money quickly. By nighttime my brain had become a graveyard of half-grown ideas that I had tried out and rejected.

Stoop-sitting with my murky thoughts for company, I didn't hear Ferdie the first time that he spoke. After he plopped down right next to me, his complaining voice finally sank in.

"That's what the newspaper says. And I say it isn't fair. Zach, you have to think of something . . . we gotta make them open it."

His complaint sounded like an echo: not enough money. Lansing Swimming Pool wasn't open yet because the city said it didn't have enough money to fix the cracks and pay the lifeguards this year.

I exploded.

"It's bad enough, Ferdie, that I can't help my own family which is in trouble, you want me to worry about the whole city of Cohoes? Listen, if this city has any money lying around, I know where it oughtta go first, and it's not into any swimming pool."

Ferdie looked shocked that I could think anything was more important than opening Lansing Pool. Since he's supposed to be my best friend and since it wasn't *our* fault we didn't have the rent money, I told him about our troubles.

"Mrs. Cusack promised to call you again for dog

training, didn't she?" Ferdie said, trying to be helpful.

"Yeah. Next Labor Day Weekend."

He fell silent after a grunted "Oh." Even Ferdie could see that fifty cents to be earned two months from now was no solution.

"I thought about hustling the *Cohoes American,* but after the last time . . . ." I shrugged without finishing my sentence.

Ferdie knew the rest because we'd gone together to the loading dock where they pass out the bundles of newspapers for guys to sell on street corners. It was in June when people were buying lots of the Extras to read about the war. Though we'd yelled out "Me, me, mister . . . give some to me" as loud as anyone there and waved our hands up high, all the papers went to grown men and big kids sixteen and seventeen years old.

Zoe, pushing and wiggling, squeezed space from between Ferdie and me to sit down. "What're you guys talking about?" she asked.

"That's for us to know and you to guess," I answered automatically. "For cryin' out loud, Zoe, there isn't room."

Naturally, she didn't leave. She only shifted to better fit herself against my side like a piece in a jigsaw puzzle, and to ask another question.

"Why does the moon grow big and then go back to teeny tiny all the time? Why's that, Zach?"

I answered her question with a question.

"Zoe, didn't Mama call you yet? What that moon in the sky means is that it's past your bedtime, never mind what size it is. C'mon."

Hauling her after me up the stairs, I wished privately that Zoe wouldn't ask me questions that I didn't know the answers to. I'd had enough of those for today.

Like a toothache, the questions with no answers were there with me when I woke up. And Zoe, too, was there with her everlasting pestering.

Handing me her shirt, she said, "Will you inside-out this for me, please? Zach, is today when we're gonna do our letters? Can I buy the stamp my ownself?"

"Not today, and no. You can't reach the stamp window."

Can you imagine the nerve of a teacher giving homework over the summer? That's what the teacher at Greek school did on the last day of school. We were to practice our Greek by writing letters over the summer to relatives or to him. He even made us all copy down his address in Pennsylvania. The last thing I needed was to be reminded of *that* assignment.

"When, Zach, when we gonna write?"

"September. September thirty-first. It's a month that's coming still."

34

"That's a big number, so it comes at the end of the month, right?"

Zoe has only a foggy notion of the months. I figured I had taken care of that one kind of neatly, at the same time paying her back for the kick in the shins.

Still stumped by our problem, I went looking for an answer in the library. Only one book in the adult section, *Secrets of Salesmen's Success,* looked like it might have something. Miss Rollins let me take it out when I said it was for my father. That was no lie, either, because Papa read the book later.

I holed up in Bonelli's to read the book. What a waste of time. The pages were filled with all these commands in capital letters and exclamation marks like: BUILD TRUST! LET THE WORLD KNOW! START DEALING AT THE TOP!! No secrets that I could see.

When the rat-tatting knocks rapped out *Shave-and-a-haircut, Two bits* on Bonelli's front door, I was more than ready to quit reading and let Ferdie in.

"Swimming pool's still closed," he announced. So the city must not have found any money between yesterday and today. Scratch one more hope.

"What are you doing?" Ferdie asked, picking up

the book and flipping pages.

"What's it look like? I'm studying ways to get my hands on some real money."

"BUY CHEAP!! SELL DEAR!!" Ferdie read out loud. "What have you got to sell?"

"Nothing yet, but even better than cheap," I said, waving my arms around at what was left of the Bonelli Electric Supply Company, "there's free stuff right here. This was a business, a real business. There must be some valuable junk to sell."

"But this is Bonelli's stuff. Not yours," Ferdie objected.

"He left it all behind. I'll be doing him a favor if I sell it, because I'd pay him a fair share after," I argued.

Half a dozen cobwebs and two splinters later, I realized I wasn't going to have any opportunity of doing Bonelli a favor. The bits of wire were too small and too few, the nails rusty and bent. There was nothing, absolutely nothing I could take to the junkyard.

"Too bad, Zach, you can't just . . . y'know . . . ZAP! and find a gold mine somewhere. I guess— in case you have to move—it's . . . uh . . . time to take this with me," said Ferdie, packing up his Monopoly and leaving.

Who needs a friend that acts like you might skip town with his belongings? Not me. I was glad— really glad, I tell you—to see Ferdie go.

A minute later, Zoe erupted into Bonelli's like an angry cat, one that tried to use me for a tree. I grabbed both of her fists and held her off while she kicked and stormed.

"Liar . . . cheat. . . . There's no thirty-one. Mama showed me. An' Setember comes way after summer's all done."

Zoe's attack didn't worry me nearly so much as Mama's voice, which was calling "*Zaharia . . . ela etho*" in a very demanding tone. I warned Zoe, "Mama's calling me to come. You better stop hitting and kicking. You'll get it if I tell her."

Not that I'd ever tell. That's too much like squealing. But my warning at least stopped Zoe from chasing after me. The way Mama grilled me about the homework that I'd "forgotten to mention" and what I had told Zoe, you'd have thought I had committed a capital crime, like murder.

"Not to do the work. The shame of it! Why do you think we pay the church two dollars every month for Greek lessons?"

Good question. Why did we? I sure never *asked* for any Greek lessons! As she drew breath for her next scold, I spoke up quickly. "Say, Mama, maybe I shouldn't go to Greek school this fall? I know enough Greek now, and we sure could use the money that we'd save."

My face almost split with a grin as I thought about all the free time I'd have if I didn't go to

Greek school every day after American school. Forcing a frown, I offered again, "I'm willing to quit."

"That you are willing to quit *all* your responsibilities is very plain, *Zaharia*," Mama said in a grim voice. "Since you know so much Greek, you will do a letter for yourself right now and help Zoe to write hers. I'm sure it won't take such an expert as yourself very long."

I groaned out loud. Anybody who's ever seen Greek knows how hard it is. It's not only that the letters are shaped differently; it's all those accent marks on top of the words that you have to get exactly right. Why, if you move just one little accent mark in a word like *podia,* it changes the word completely. Instead of *feet,* all of a sudden it means *apron.* How can you write fast in a language like that?

Zoe and I worked at the last table, the one our family usually eats at, so we were right there when Papa came in the front door of the Miss Liberty.

Mama's eyebrows went up in a questioning way, and I stopped dead in the middle of hunting through the dictionary.

"I asked." Papa spoke slowly. "I asked at the bank. . . ."

"And?"

"And the president is taking his holiday for a month."

Mama's eyebrows pulled together in a frown and her shoulders slumped.

"Did you show anyone the slips, the total of what is owing us?"

"To no purpose. The clerk behind the window bars says it is no part of his job to make decisions."

I couldn't keep myself from their conversation any longer. "What you have to do, Papa, is to tell him . . . ."

"Zach, you are of an age to be informed, but not yet old enough to make the plans or to command this family," Papa said, cutting me off angrily.

Holy Nellie, he didn't have to yell. I only wanted to help.

"*Zaharia,* you are a smart boy but still you are only a boy. Don't lose your sleep over this," Mama said gently.

"Yeah, well, if I saw that bank president, I could tell him what a Grade A rat he was. If his bank burned down . . . ."

"*Zaharia!* Watch your tongue, especially what you say outside to other people. And don't you dare get any ideas," Mama warned.

I was struck dumb for a whole five seconds.

"Mama, give me credit for *some* sense! I'm not gonna set any fires, and I'm not gonna broadcast our trouble to the world." (I don't count Ferdie Gaudet as the world.) "Anyway, America's the country of free speech, remember? Even if I did say that the bank stinks, or spoke up to the president, nobody would put me in jail. Everybody here is equal, you know."

That's when Zoe butted in to ask if we could go now to the post office with our letters.

Mama, who had started brushing Zoe's hair, stopped suddenly with the brush in midair. She gave a funny answer, funny because Mama never ever puts anything off. "Wait. Wait till the end of the day. Or better, tomorrow."

That was the first but not the last surprise. After breakfast the next day, she asked me to help her with a little writing. That's not the surprising part. I help Mama a couple of times a week because she's studying to pass the test and become an American citizen.

No, the surprise was having her call me to come *upstairs* to work at our dining room table instead of at the family table in the store. More surprising still were the two pages on the table already written out. Both were in Greek. Was she writing to the Greek school teacher, too?

I must have said that out loud, because Mama, whose cheeks looked red, answered me.

"Not to *Kyrie* Karolaftis. But I wrote in Greek first to get it all in order. Now you will help me to translate and write correctly in English."

It was what you might call a business letter, but when we changed the Greek exactly into English, it didn't sound quite right. I got the library book about business to show her what I meant.

"If you want to practice American-style business letters, I think you should change some of it. Start it the way they do here, Mama."

"No, that's not respectful enough," said Mama.

Well, when I thought about who she was addressing in the letter, I suppose she was right. So the opening—"Most Respected and Dearly Beloved President and Mrs. Franklin Delano Roosevelt"—stayed the same.

Then she went on to say: "The knowledge that you are trying to help *all* Americans, farmers and city people, has made me bold to write to you. I know you are burdened with many letters, so I will be brief."

The way she laid out facts and figures after that was just like a lawyer. Her last sentence thanked him for giving us the high honor of taking part in the Works Program for the relief of poor people.

"You write more quickly than I, *Zaharia,* so make a copy in your best handwriting to send, and another copy for ourselves to keep."

"Mama, I thought you were just *practicing.* You're not serious? You can't send that letter for real to President Roosevelt."

"Why not?"

"Why . . . why, because he's got so much to worry about, like the defense effort and running again

41

for President. He can't take time to do anything about our trouble."

"Don't I read in the newspaper all the time how the *Proedros* is asking for advice on how the government can better serve the people? I'm telling him just that. He must send quickly the money we have earned. And if he's too busy, the *Proedrina*, Mrs. Roosevelt, will take care of it."

Nothing I said budged Mama from her determination to send the letter. Debts had to be paid, she said, and the U.S. government was wrong to take so long in paying its bills.

Before going back to work downstairs, Mama gave me stamp money and said, "Don't take Zoe to the post office with you. Oh, and Zach, until we see a reply, let's keep this a . . . like a little secret between the two of us. After all, a rooster who crows in the night has trouble finding hens."

I didn't understand the last sentence but I said amen to the first part. The fewer people who knew, the less the chance of our being laughed at.

As long as I was truly stuck with this job, I figured I might as well do it right. Carefully, very carefully, I wrote July 7 at the top of the first page. We had no carbon paper to make copies for the "interested parties" the way it said in the business book, so I had to write out Mama's letter five times altogether.

At the post office, I realized suddenly that the change purse didn't have enough money. My own fault, I guess, for not explaining to Mama about having to make and mail all those other copies, too. Lucky I had my whole quarter with me. I used that.

The expression on the clerk's face as he read the White House address made me mad, so I told him to send that one special delivery. Paying out nine cents for mailing three copies plus an extra dime for the special delivery was just like dropping money into a slot machine that's been fixed. There's no way to pull your money back out of the slot and no way that you can win any money, either.

Still feeling kind of reckless, I stopped at La Marche's and bought a twin-stick Fudgsicle, saving one half for Zoe. What the heck. The six cents change from my quarter couldn't make any difference in what we owed the bank. The last penny went for a double bubblegum.

Nothing seemed to matter anymore. Ferdie came over, and I didn't even try to talk him into bringing his Monopoly back. Each day dragged like a dinosaur's tail. I didn't see how Papa could keep on looking so cheerful as he waited on customers.

"You better believe it that times are getting better," said Mr. Rubenstein. He owns a factory across the street. "I sent a double order of dresses last Friday to New York."

Nodding agreement, Papa added, "Pete Flanagan tells me two more cars of garnets coming through every week on the freight from the mines up north. Business is picking up all over."

Papa was just kidding himself if he thought we were going to have a happy ending. He knew—and I knew—that we couldn't wait for this prosperity to trickle down to us.

But Papa's conversation with Rubenstein must have planted a seed in my head, and, like Jack's beanstalk, it blossomed overnight. *I woke up with a solution,* full grown. It's a good thing I'm in the habit of reading our social studies books all the way through, even the parts that aren't assigned.

After double checking in my last year's book, I called Ferdie and Karl to a meeting up in the Big Woods where we could have privacy and no Zoe. Georgie La Rouche is too small and talks too much, so I didn't include him.

Bringing Karl up to date on the Miss Liberty's cash problems, I finished with, "So we need buckets of money in a hurry. I know where to get some and if you guys will help me, I'll give you a share."

They agreed. I figured they would. After I made each swear on his honor not to tell another living human being what we were about to do, I asked,

"Either of you guys know what a garnet is?"

"A stone, isn't it? One that you have to dig up?" Karl guessed.

"A semiprecious stone," I informed them, emphasizing the precious. I gave them the next question. "Do you know what passes through Cohoes every week?"

Ferdie, who doesn't like to overwork his brain, shuffled impatiently and said, "Are we going to help you, or d'you want to play Twenty Questions?"

Ignoring him, I answered my own question. "Carloads of garnets from the Adirondack Mountains. That's what passes through Cohoes every week on the freight trains. *Carloads of semiprecious stones.*"

The expression on their faces told me they could hardly believe their ears. Karl, the first to recover, asked cautiously, "But how is that fact going to help the Miss Liberty, Zach?"

"Semiprecious stones are like jewels, so they're worth a lot of money. What we're going to do is sell them and get that money."

"You never . . . Zach, you never mean to say you wanna *rob* the train?"

Ferdie's voice had risen to a high squawk like a chicken whose head was about to be cut off. Good thing we were in the Big Woods where nobody could hear us.

"*No!*" I shook my head in disgust. "We don't have to rob anybody or anything. Use your head for something besides a hat rack, Ferdie. Think. What happens when coal cars pass through? Pieces fly off, fall out on the tracks, right? Everybody knows the rule: Finders, keepers; losers, weepers. That's why in the fall you see people walking along the track filling up sacks with those pieces of coal for their stoves. So-oo, if an open freight car has garnets, why then . . . ."

Ferdie, his Adam's apple bobbing like a yo-yo with excitement, came up with a strangled "Wowee," while Karl murmured "Fan-tastic."

Then, cautious as ever, Karl asked, "How come nobody else has noticed that this valuable stuff is passing right under their noses?"

I dredged up an answer for him out of my memory bank. "I guess because it's in the form of ore. We'll probably have to break down the pieces."

Karl offered to bring a meat hammer from his father's meat market. We needed something to put the stones in and Ferdie thought he could get a pail, maybe two of them, from his pa's saloon without anybody noticing.

"Gee, Zach, I could almost believe you said ZAP! and called up Super Powers to figure this one out," said Karl.

It was too good a chance to pass up. I let the corner of my mouth curve up in a half smile like someone who knows a secret but isn't telling. No-tice I didn't *say* I had super powers, since I make it a habit not to lie.

"Maybe, maybe when we pick up the ore, we'll find gold, too," said Ferdie, spraying us with drops of his excited breath.

Trust Ferdie to want more than one fortune!

I'm pretty sure you don't find gold in the same rocks as garnets but I didn't say anything. I only warned them both that we'd have to go after dark. "We don't want anyone else to butt into our deal, and besides, you know how they always chase us kids away from the railroad tracks. We got lots of candle stubs at my house left over from Easter time at church. I'll bring those, so we can see to hunt."

We headed home to get ready for the night's work. Karl split off at the corner of Remsen, and Ferdie turned in at the Ladies' Entrance at the side of the saloon, while I jogged on up Mohawk Street.

The sight of the three men standing at the foot of the Miss Liberty's steps slowed my feet to a crawl. But my heartbeat speeded up to double-time. Anybody could tell these men weren't regular customers. Our regulars don't wear pin-striped suits and high-collared white shirts with fat ties. The only one of the three I recognized was Mayor Roulier, and his face looked churchy serious. The men were just finishing their good-bys to Papa and Mama, who stood on the top step of the Miss Liberty.

I felt the way you do when your foot's been asleep and comes awake: all shooting, prickly pains. Naturally, I didn't cry, but as the men started down the street, I stuck my tongue out at their backs. Mama saw me and gave a quick, disapproving *tcch,* but I didn't care.

What right did these big shots have to come? It wasn't the end of July yet. And I was so close. I was so close to getting my hands on money for the rent. Hoping and at the same time dreading to find out what was going on, I followed Papa and Mama into the store.

Mama, who gets a lot of comfort from a cup of coffee, had already filled a mug and stopped at the end of the counter by the sugar bowl. She wore a dazed look like the one that Ferdie got when he'd been hit with a fly ball.

"I don't understand what brought those men to us and why the one from the newspaper wants to write a story. I wrote only the one letter to President Roosevelt. For that matter, the letter to our *Proedros* has scarcely had time to reach Washington. And Mayor Roulier . . . ." Mama shook her head in puzzlement. "To say that he will himself bring us the money just as if he is an errand boy. I don't understand."

Papa exhaled strongly, a long breath that lifted the ends of his mustache. "My dear, we need to understand only one thing: that the bank president insists that he wouldn't dream of evicting such good, hard-working citizens as ourselves."

Papa laughed and hugged Mama so hard that her coffee went sloshing. Then he gave a little jump in the air and slapped the heel of his shoe, the way Greek men do when they lead a line of dancers. We all burst out laughing.

Everybody sobered up fast at the sight of the letter that came in the afternoon mail. It had the White House seal on the top left-hand corner of the envelope. Papa read the letter aloud slowly.

The Assistant Secretary to the President acknowledged receipt of our special delivery letter and informed us that the Administrator of Public Works had been ordered to resolve the matter promptly.

The last paragraph said, "Kindly permit me to take this opportunity also of commending your participation in the President's Relief Program and to tell you that he sincerely appreciates your cooperation."

Below his signature was a list of all those who got carbon copies. The bank and the others must have received theirs in the morning mail.

After studying it for a minute more in silence, Papa suddenly turned to me and said, "I detect

your helping hand in here somewhere, *Zaharia*. What did you add to your mother's letter?"

"Nothing, Papa, honestly. I wrote just what Mama told me. I used my own dime for the special delivery. And, like the business book said, I made copies for all the 'interested parties.' One for the bank, of course, and one for the mayor. I figured the newspaper is always writing about the President and his programs, so they should get one, too."

Papa gave a great shout of laughter that rumbled down to short bursts of chuckles. In between those, he said, "LET THE WORLD KNOW. START DEALING AT THE TOP. Oh, Zach, you learned the lessons in that book very well indeed. We must find money for a frame and hang this behind the cash register."

Zoe wants to frame her letter from the Greek school teacher, too. It came in the same mail. She keeps nagging me to listen, especially to the sentence about her being a pupil who shines like the evening star with bright promise, and the closing that said, "Your loving teacher."

At bedtime, she asked, "Zach, can you keep a secret?"

I groaned out loud and pulled the pillow over my head.

"You'll have to keep it for a long, long time," Zoe warned.

Whether I wanted to hear it or not, she was determined to tell me. Tugging the pillow corner off, she leaned over and whispered in my ear.

"I love *Kyrie* Karolaftis, too. When I grow up, I'm gonna marry him and live in Altoona."

"Zoe, that's an easy one. I can keep that secret forever," I promised.

Too bad I can't keep what Papa told me a secret, too. That ore from Gore Mountain, he says, is what they call industrial grade ore. Behr-Manning powders it and makes cloths that polish gun barrels. It's not ever used for making jewelry.

All I've done so far is call off the garnet hunt for tonight. Ferdie took the postponement all right, but his heart is gonna break when he finds out tomorrow that it's off permanently. Still, it's his own fault. He shouldn't have been so foolish as to think he could find treasure in Cohoes, New York.

3

The New-Style Holiday

"Wanna play catch?"

"Ball's flat."

"How about Cops and Robbers?" asked Ferdie, trying again.

"Not enough guys."

Ferdie scratched his head and finally, having reached a conclusion, he shared it. "That means there's nothing to do, right?"

"That's right."

Then he waited, looking at me expectantly. That Ferdie has no idea what to do with himself unless I tell him. I buttoned my lip. Since I was dying of boredom, I didn't see why he should go scot-free.

When Ferdie saw I wasn't going to rescue him with some great idea, he got up from the step and left with a mumbled "See ya."

Ever since the Fourth, the summer has seemed more and more like a boring book that I've read before. You might think that Zoe's and my birthdays would put a little excitement into this week, at least. Hers is today and mine is two days from now.

It's a funny-peculiar, not a ha-ha-funny, thing: Our being in the same family and having birthdays so close on the calendar, you'd think we would look alike. But my skin is light and my hair so close to blond that strangers never believe we're brother and sister.

That isn't the only odd thing about us Poulos kids and our birthdays. In our house nothing happens on birthdays. They're just like any other day.

"Zach, how far do I have to go before I get to China?"

"Huh?"

"I said, how far do I have to dig? How long will it take me to get to China?" Zoe yelled from the curb. Her yellow sunsuit was fast turning brown because she was sitting on the dirt square where the cement sidewalk is missing. Dirt flew left and right as she dug with an old rusty spoon in the middle of the square.

"A long, long time. After you go down to the middle of the earth where Hell and the Devil are, and you get through all the flames and the snakes, then you have to dig through the other half."

"I don't believe you. You're just saying that to be mean."

I shrugged. She was right, but I felt like being mean today.

"Zach? Zachary Athanasius . . . ."

Zoe's voice sounded a little quavery. She stood up suddenly and backed away from the dirt square.

"Zach, I . . . *you* fill up the hole," and in a rush she'd gone past me, banging the screen door of the Miss Liberty.

Zoe's not one to back off from things, so I got up from the stoop and strolled over to the curb to see. Humping its way out of the deep hole that Zoe had dug was a huge, brown, fat, wiggling worm.

"Hurry, Zach. Hurry!" With her face pressed up against the screen and nose flattened, Zoe shouted, "He'll get free and then the big snakes 'n' then . . . ."

That did it. All this morning I thought I'd never even smile again, but Zoe made me laugh out loud. Seeing the worm right after what I had said must have convinced her that the Devil himself was coming next.

"He's gone, gone. I dashed his brains out, Zoe," I called to her after tossing the worm into the road. Because she was so scared, I kicked a little dirt into the hole before going back to sit on the bottom step where I resumed thinking.

Being Greek in America sometimes makes me feel like I'm riding two horses at once, each going in a different direction. It gives a person a strange feeling, let me tell you, to be the only family around that doesn't celebrate birthdays.

Greeks celebrate name days instead of birthdays. That's the day of the saint that you're named after. If my name day falls on a Sunday and we go to church over in Troy, some people will shake my hand, leaving a quarter—or once fifty cents—in my palm as a present. It's the custom to treat kids on their name day. But if it comes on a weekday, forget it. All I get is kisses and good wishes from Papa and Mama. Just once, I'd like to blow out some candles on a birthday cake.

Squealing Zoe's name, Monique Gaudet came out from next door practically head first. She ran over to ask, "Where's Zoe? My mama says on accounta it's her birthday, you can come for lunch."

"Oh, I didn't know you cared, Monkey Monique. You want *me*? Can't Zoe come, too?"

"Silly. You *and* Zoe, Mama said. Hurry."

I don't know why I waste my time and talents kidding little squirts like Monique. They don't recognize a joke unless it stands up and bites them.

After we came back home, I told Papa, who was chopping onions for the Coney Island Sauce, about the party that Mrs. Gaudet had made for us.

"Sandwiches with *two* slices bologna in each, and she cut them fancy, into quarters. We had Pepsi and chocolate cupcakes after that, and she wore her Sunday apron."

I looked over my shoulder from the sink where I was washing the dishes to see what Papa thought of it. He was frowning, but I think it was from the onions and not because a stranger had made a birthday party for his kids.

Maybe I'd have better luck with Mama. She would surely be impressed when she saw the hand-kerchiefs we'd gotten from the Gaudets. Zoe's had lace on the edges. Ferdie's Tante Marie had made the lace herself and had embroidered Z A P on mine by hand. Normally, I don't count clothes as a present, but I never before had something with my initials on it.

I found Mama by the front door saying good-by to Mustaki, a Greek from Albany. He comes to visit every so often and brings Mama up to date on news of other Greeks.

"Yes, yes. Lovely. So kind," she murmured, feeling the handkerchief that I showed her, but plainly, her mind was elsewhere.

"When people come from someplace else—like, say, Ferdie's family from Canada—they oughtta do like everybody else does in the new country. At least, that's what the Gaudets think about birth-days, anyway. What d'you think, Mama?"

She didn't really answer me, much less get the hint.

"Oh, *Zaharia,* I have many more serious things to think about just now. I must talk with Papa," Mama said, heading abruptly for the kitchen.

Boy! Putting an idea in Papa or Mama's head

was certainly lots harder than planting one in Ferdie's. The more I thought about it, though, the madder I got at Mama. After all, what could be more serious than being born?

Zoe's decided already that having a birthday is even better than going to a carnival. She told me at bedtime that on account of her birthday she'd been invited to lunch again, the next day at Anna Bobkov's house.

Bobkov is our milkman, but we know him from Russian church, too. Some Sundays, instead of going to Greek church over in Troy, we go down the street to St. Nicholas. It's an Orthodox church like ours. People there do everything the same as Greeks do except they do it all in Russian.

Anna, who's an only child, comes in to the city with her father sometimes and plays with Zoe while he does his milk route.

"It's a real farm with *live* cows 'n' everything, Mama says. I've never been so far before. I'm glad I'm six years old," Zoe informed me.

"Five," I said, correcting her automatically.

"But this birthday finishes the five years since I was born. I'm already starting six years tomorrow," Zoe argued.

"That's counting the Greek way. You were born here, so start acting American," I said crossly. "Shut up and go to sleep."

"I know what. You're jealous. That's what.

'Cause I'm having lots of parties."

"Jealous? Of what? Of you chewing with the cows? Don't make me laugh."

Mama, coming in to kiss Zoe good-night, said, "But Zach doesn't have to be jealous at all. He'll be going with you."

"*Wha-at?*" I came bolt upright from the bed where I'd been trying to read. "I'm not gonna spend the day playing with a couple of five-year-olds. No, sirree!"

"You will," said Mama sternly. "It's the only way I can permit her to go. A farmer's wife has too much work to watch over two little girls all day while they play. No more 'shut ups,' either, to Zoe or anyone else, *Zaharia*. That's rude talk."

I tried again in the morning, pointing out to Papa that I couldn't do my chores if I went away for the day.

"Such a sense of responsibility, Zach," Papa answered. "I'm impressed. But just this once, I think your mother or I can manage to do the dishes. You're so concerned about the customs of this country, you can think of this day as your birthday gift to Zoe," he added.

I think he was being what you call sarcastic, but I made up my mind that nobody was going to have any reason to call me stingy. I got my pride. I didn't even take a book with me to read.

Good thing I had both hands free when we left

with Bobkov. The milk wagon has only one seat, on the driver's side, so I rode standing up with one foot inside and one foot on the fender. The door on my side stays slid back to let him jump down quickly with milk bottles. I balanced myself by holding on to the door frame with both hands, but there was no real worry about falling off. Dama, his horse, clip-clops very slowly. Zoe sat on top of a turned-over milk crate on the floor between Bobkov and me.

From my stand-up position, I could see way ahead, except that there was less and less to see as we wound our way up the hill. Fewer and fewer houses, farther and farther apart, until it was nothing but grass and trees. So much grass stuff that it made the air smell different. Different but okay. It sure beat the stink waves that come off the canals in the city in summertime.

Mr. Bobkov laughed when he saw me sniffing. "You gotta open your nose wide in the country. Get all the fresh air you can. It makes you grow," he said, looking over at me. "I hear you, too, gonna have a birthday. How old?"

"Twelve tomorrow."

"A man, almost," Bobkov said.

We stopped finally to turn in at a barn that was right at the side of the road. Anna, who was waiting in the barnyard, shouted for Zoe to jump down. The two hugged and bounced around one another like a couple of goofy golf balls, then ran up the curving path and disappeared in a tunnel of trees.

"Don't worry. Anna is only taking Zoe up to the house," said Mr. Bobkov.

I had too many other things on my mind—like the terrific hiding places I saw all around—to even think about Zoe.

"You can help me unload the crates and put Dama into her stall," he added, with one eyebrow raised in a questioning way.

I could tell he thought I was too short and skinny to be much help. Still, he didn't take it back, and the job of unhitching Dama's bridle and reins was better than any game I ever thought up.

Bobkov let me do it all by myself, too. Lucky I watch pretty closely when I go to the movies so I knew which end to start at. Helping Bobkov with the crates of empty bottles didn't raise any problems; I move soda crates every day to fill the cooler in the Miss Liberty.

"You got more muscle than I thought, boy. It's time now to join with the girls."

For cryin' out loud, after all I'd done, how could Bobkov say that? I wiped the sweat off my forehead with the back of my arm. You'd think he would recognize that I belonged here, doing men's work.

"They need someone big with them. Swimming—especially down there," said Mr. Bobkov, jerking his head to the left of the barn, "can be dangerous."

"You got a swimming pool here?" I asked in amazement.

"A crick, one with fast running water. In some places, it got potholes, too. Scary for Zoe 'cause she's so little. And Anna is not so steady jumping on the rocks in the shallow parts. Without you, they can't play in the crick, so go now."

Wow! Going in the water would be a real treat. We haven't been swimming once this summer because of Lansing Pool being closed. Then I remembered. "Can't, Mr. Bobkov," I said glumly. "We didn't bring any bathing suits."

Mr. Bobkov, reaching in under the driver's seat of the wagon, pulled out a black wool bag with a design of bright zigzags on one side. It was Mama's shopping bag.

"Your mama planned for this trip," he said with a smile, tossing the bag to me. "Yours and Zoe's suits are in there."

I let the girls chase me all over the farm first. Then we went into the creek to cool off. What a difference from swimming in a pool! In a creek you never know where the bottom is going to be, and there are so many other live things in there with you.

I made believe I was Tarzan of the Apes, only instead of swinging, I jumped from the branch of a tree over the narrow part of the creek to the other side. Zoe, who can be a smart cookie sometimes, got the brilliant idea of building a dam. It made a deeper pool. When the girls stood in the dammed-up narrow part, the water came up to Zoe's neck. That's what gave her the idea, I guess, of pretending to be a shark. She and Anna splashed and snapped their jaws at my heels every time I jumped over them.

I could hardly believe it when Mrs. Bobkov called us in. It seemed like only a minute since we'd finished lunch and gone to explore the barn. But I had plenty of room for the cookies and milk that she put out. Did you ever taste milk fresh from the cow? I don't know whether it's because of the pail or what, but it tastes different, sweeter somehow. Even Zoe drank a full glass.

That's when Anna gave Zoe a birthday present: a box of sixteen colored pencils, brand new, with shades like maroon and navy. There was a knobby-hard, kind of funny-shaped package wrapped in white tissue paper for me, too.

"Do you know what it is?" asked Mrs. Bobkov anxiously after I'd unwrapped it.

I nodded, speechless for a minute. "Well, it's . . . yes, well . . . but are you sure you want to give them to me? Aren't they too valuable?"

"But you have been valuable, too. A help to the mister and good to the little girls. Our Anna does not care much for these, so we decided you should have them. We find such things often on the farm here. If you want to make a collection, we can add more by-and-by."

If I wanted. What a question! Even Karl Schmidt, who's so proud of his model airplanes, would give his right arm to have *genuine* Indian arrowheads. These three were beauties, and I bet that they're worth more than their weight in gold.

That night I didn't go out after supper; I worked instead on a case to hold my present. I drew a border of Indian-like designs on a piece of paper, and after I colored it with Zoe's pencils, I pasted this new lining in my cigar box. Then I put each arrowhead on a little pillow of cotton and covered them all with my new handkerchief before I shut the lid. I couldn't wait to show the kids my arrowheads. I was still grinning to myself when I fell asleep.

"Zach-jack . . . Zach-jack . . . *Zaharia . . . Hronia Polla, Zaharia . . . .*"

The silly rhyme was spilling into my left ear while the Greek drifted down from somewhere on my right. Something—a moth? a kiss?—brushed each cheek, and laughter followed.

Zoe, straddling my chest and tugging my hand, pulled me out of a deep sleep, saying, "Happy birthday, Lazy Bones."

"*Hronia Polla,*" Mama, on my right, repeated. "*Na ta ekatostisis.*"

A Happy Birthday wish I can understand, but why would anyone want to live to be a hundred, I wondered. Especially when a birthday is like every other day. Actually, I ought to take that back. Mama doesn't normally wake me up. She had something in her hand, too, I noticed, so I sat up quickly.

"As it's your birthday, *Zaharia,* I let you sleep late. But it's time now and you must put something on the sunburn before your nose pains you. Here, rub the Vaseline on good and thick before your breakfast, not after," said Mama.

The Vaseline helped my nose but not much else. I had the letdown feeling all through breakfast, even though Papa said I could have as many jelly doughnuts as I wanted this once. I ate only two.

Of course, I know better than to expect real birthday presents, but you'd think that at least I'd have a day off today. No such luck. Although it was late in the morning, all the dirty breakfast dishes were there, waiting as usual for me to wash them.

The job was just bearable because I kept my mind on how I would pull off the handkerchief and show my arrowheads to Ferdie and Karl and Georgie. Dishes done, I tore out of the store and down the alley between Gaudets' and our house to find the guys. With six houses sharing the same backyard, everybody more or less makes the yard headquarters for meeting.

The gang was there, all right, huddled in one corner, everybody talking at the same time. Georgie La Rouche, who spotted me, poked his head back into the huddle and said something. Suddenly they all stopped talking. I looked back over my shoulder to see if maybe a grownup had come down the alley behind me, but nobody had.

"Hey, guys, have I got something to show you!" I yelled. "Let's call a meeting of the club." We pretty much have a club going all the time. I make up the passwords, and usually I write the rules.

"Can't," said Georgie, as I got to them. "My mother wants me home. We're gonna eat."

"But it's not lunchtime," I objected.

"I can't help that. What she said was I had to get there right away." And Georgie took off down the alley.

When I looked around, Ferdie was drifting over to his back porch stairs, and Karl to the back fence that he climbs over to get home.

"Well, you guys don't have to go anywhere," I said.

"Yes, I do," Ferdie answered quickly. "I just remembered. I gotta go to the store to get something."

"Shopping?" I couldn't believe my ears. "Okay.

66

So I'll go with you. Did y'hear I drove a horse yesterday? No lie. Bobkov let me take the reins coming home from the farm. When we get back from the store, I want to show you something super special."

"You can't. I mean you can't come with me," Ferdie blurted. "This shopping is . . . uh . . . for my pa and he doesn't want anybody . . . uh . . . knowing our business."

Ferdie's Adam's apple was bouncing up and down like a yo-yo, the way it does when he gets excited—*or* when he's lying. Nobody has to hit me over the head with a baseball bat to make a point.

"Karl?" I asked, turning to him to see what excuse he would make.

Karl, who was practically over the fence already, sent Ferdie a look. I know that kind of look. I've used it myself when there's a pest around. It says: After we get rid of him, let's get back together.

"Sorry, Zach. I promised to clean my room." With that he disappeared over the other side, as Ferdie raced up the stairs to his back porch.

I got this creepy feeling that I was a live, walking advertisement. You know: the one where a guy comes in the room and everybody clears out because he has B.O. and not even his best friend will tell him.

The bathroom is the only place where I can be

certain that Zoe won't barge in on me, so I headed there. I had to be sure. Locking the door I lifted up my arms, left and right, and sniffed my armpits. Nothing. I mean I smelled the same as I always do. The most that I could pick out was a little whiff of Octagon soap.

Wait, I said to myself, just wait till the next time that Ferdie wants somebody to hang out with, or Karl needs me to help glue his model airplanes. They'd find it easier to nail Jell-O to a tree than to get ahold of me.

All afternoon I kept a sharp lookout for the guys, so I could walk away from them, the way I planned. But I never saw or heard anybody in the backyard or even down on the corner. For once, I didn't feel like reading; instead, I hunted for Zoe, tracking her by the notes of "Jingle Bells." It's the one song she knows by heart, so she sings it all year long.

"Zoe, I'll play you a game of cards. Go Fish, if you like," I offered as I came up to the doorway of our bedroom.

Bang. The door slammed shut in my face, and Zoe on the other side shrieked, "Go away, Zach. Far, far 'way. You can't come in."

Even Zoe! I could force the door open, but what's the use?

"Hope your insides stick together the next time you swallow your chewing gum," I said, but softly under my breath so she couldn't run squealing to

Mama that I had wished she'd die.

Like rubbing a lamp to bring a genie, my thinking about Mama brought her at that moment to the head of the stairs.

"*Zaharia,* you must go to the *neife*'s house. This whole week we haven't asked if she needs anything."

Nick Stangos, who has the Pilgrim Lunch on Remsen Street, brought a bride all the way from Greece this spring. His *neife* is young and homesick a lot, so Mama tries to keep an eye on her. She took Katerina to the five-and-ten-cent store, shopping, and explained how things work with electricity and all. But the chief errand boy and messenger is me, naturally.

On the walk over to the Stangoses' house, I made up my mind. Pretty soon, Papa and Mama would have to do their own errands and the dishes because I was going to move out. Huck Finn was my age when he took off, and he made out all right. If I saved a little money, by my birthday next year I could get away from here. Maybe they'd even be a little bit sorry when I was gone.

I had a surprise when Katerina opened the door. She was licking white powder off her fingers and the house smelled like a bakery. Usually, I find her winding up the Victrola to play the same Greek record over and over while she weeps a little.

Still, like everybody else I met today, she looked at me with a frown and said, "Oh, *Zaharia*. Can't you go away for a bit?"

You'd think on a person's birthday, *somebody* would look glad to see him.

She must have seen something in my expression because quickly she swung the door wide and invited me in. Leading me into the kitchen, she explained, "It's not you, *Zaharia*. It's the stove I'm mad at. The last tray of *kourabiedes* is not done yet. I wish I had a good stone oven instead of this peculiar American stove."

My mouth started watering so much that I was afraid to open it to talk. *Kourabiedes* are my very favorite cookie. Crumbly, buttery, snowed-over with powdered sugar, they melt—really and truly melt—in your mouth. They cost a lot of money to make, so usually they're saved for visitors or special occasions.

"Tell Mama I am following her advice about keeping occupied," she said, waving her hand at the finished tray on the table. "But see how flat and spread out these are. I must need to practice more."

"I'll bet they taste okay. Y'want me to try one and tell you?" I offered.

"Do you think one would be enough to tell?" she asked with a little grin.

The two of us ate three apiece while I explained

to her about celebrating birthdays with presents. I told her that mine was today; she figured out that her eighteenth birthday, her last one, was on the day she arrived in America.

"I like this giving of presents. Tell you what, *Zaharia*. These *kourabiedes* are not worthy of being gifts, but since this is your day, take them all with you. Next week I'll bake again. Come back then for a better batch more suitable to be a gift."

Wowee! *Kourabiedes* last a long time without going stale. At this rate I was getting practically a year's supply! And they would last at least that long because I certainly didn't intend to give any of my so-called friends a one.

I helped Katerina sift powdered sugar over the last tray and pack them in a cardboard box. I set out for home, walking slowly and carefully. As soon as I turned the corner onto Mohawk, I saw Papa, who had come halfway down the block to meet me.

"Go to the Capitol Restaurant. Here's money and the number to call in Albany. Mustaki will answer the phone. Tell him your father will be there on Sunday to finish the deal. Remember: Tell him your father says yes. We'll take it over by August seventh."

I hadn't even finished one errand, and here he was with another for me already! "What are you taking over? First, can I put my box . . . ."

"No, and later. I'll explain later," Papa promised. Taking the box from me, he shooed me off down the street.

The counterman at the Capitol offered to make the call for me, but I said no, thank you, even though I had to stretch a little to reach the mouthpiece on the wall. I was as quick and businesslike as I could be.

"You must be older than you look," said the counterman after I hung up.

"Twelve. Today," I answered shortly, but I was pleased that he could tell I wasn't a little kid.

"Y'don't say. Happy Birthday, kid." Smiling, he picked up a packet of Dentyne chewing gum from the carton by the cash register and tossed it at me. "Here, catch. Have one on me in honor of the day."

My answering smile faded as I made my way home. When I counted it up, I had never before gotten so many presents in my whole life: the handkerchief, the arrowheads, the *kourabiedes*, and now the gum. Still, I felt kind of rotten. If all the grownups who weren't even my friends helped me to celebrate, how come my own family and best friends couldn't be bothered?

As I entered the Miss Liberty, Papa called out, "Oh, Zach, one more thing: Your friends . . . ."

I couldn't bear it.

"*No!* I can't do one more thing. I'm going to the bathroom. And besides, I don't have any friends."

72

"Surprise! Happy . . . Surprise! . . . Birthday . . . Zach . . . ."

Like some kind of waterfall, shouting kids came pouring out of the kitchen into the front of the store: Ferdie wearing a new polo shirt, Georgie all dressed up in the white shirt that he uses for Sunday School. Zoe and her friends were all there, too: Monique, Anna and Meggie from Zoe's kindergarten class.

That's why Papa had blocked my way into the store earlier!

"Are you surprised?" asked Georgie.

"He must be. He's not saying anything. The day that Zach doesn't have anything to say is a miracle day," said Karl, chortling and chuckling.

Mama looked a little anxious as she said, "You shared in Zoe's celebrations, so I hope you don't mind if she celebrates, too, though it's truly your party."

"Heck, no, Mama."

I could barely get the words out over the lump in my throat. Opening my presents, I whistled when I saw the beautiful, hard-maple yo-yo Ferdie had given me. It came with two extra strings and a sheet of instructions that showed you how to do "Walking My Baby Back Home" and the "World's Fair."

"I thought I'd croak when you said you'd go shopping with me. I couldn't let you pick out your own present, could I? Didn't I pick a good one for you?" asked Ferdie.

"Your pa asked me to pass the word around about the party for you and Zoe. You never caught on, did you?" Georgie La Rouche bragged. "C'mon, open mine next. If you've read them, you can trade them back in."

I hadn't read a single one of the comic books, and even if I had, I wouldn't take them back. A present is a present. Karl gave me a stamp album, the jumbo one so I'd never run out of spaces for my stamps. Even Zoe had a present for me. She'd spent the afternoon drawing a picture of our day in the country. Her cow had three legs, but I agreed that it was the best she'd ever drawn.

Last but best was Papa and Mama's present: a jackknife with five attachments, including the saw blade and the screwdriver. My old jackknife had only one blade and that had a nick in it.

Papa, carrying in platters from the kitchen, smiled when I stuttered my thanks. He set the platters one on each table and said, "A good *American* knife for a hard-working *American* boy."

Mama, right behind him with two bowls, said, "Time now for eats. We have today, in honor of the birthday, Zach and Zoe's favorite dishes."

Uh-uh. Too late to warn my folks and too late to get them to take the food back. Cheeks hot, I slumped down on my spine in embarrassment. Not for the first time, I wished that my folks had been born or at least grown up in this country. Poor Papa and Mama. They couldn't know that birthday party food is hot dogs like Mrs. Schmidt served or cake and popcorn like Georgie's mother had. *Not* Greek-style meatballs, and flaky *phyllo* dough wrapped around a feta cheese filling.

Papa broke the silence that followed Zoe's delighted shrieks of "Goody-goody gumdrops" by turning to Karl and asking, "What is the favorite food that your mother makes for you?"

"You mean special, not everyday?"

I sat up, curious to hear what he had to say. Pretty generally, we don't eat at one another's houses. Mama says it's an imposition and a burden for some mothers to have extra mouths to feed. Not mentioning any names, understand, but I know one person in our neighborhood who eats catsup sandwiches because there isn't any other filling to put between the bread by the end of the month.

I could hardly believe my ears when Karl answered. Maybe his mother has some secret for making it tasty, but I'd never in a million years pick liver and onions as *my* favorite food. Of course, his father is a butcher, so probably he has to eat up whatever meat is left over in the shop, the way we do with the restaurant food.

Georgie picked fried pork chops as his favorite,

but Ferdie's choice was a real stunner. He's eaten it only once at a wedding in Montreal, but he said he never forgot how good it tasted. Nobody knew what *escargot* meant, not even Georgie, so Ferdie translated from the French.

I looked at Ferdie with new respect. Anybody who willingly ate *snails* and said he loved them had guts. More guts than brains, I decided.

"Your pa and ma are good cooks," said Ferdie with a burp as he finished his second cream soda. "I like your kind of meatballs and that cheese pie— whatcha-call-it—*tiropita*."

"I could tell you did," I said.

Mama had made a packet of both for his mother and Tante Marie. If I know ol' Greedy Guts Gaudet, he'll eat most of that, too.

Papa had baked a real American-style cake, one layer strawberry frosted for Zoe and one layer chocolate frosted for me, so we each had a set of candles to blow out. Finally, I'll find out if birthday wishes really do come true. But I'll have to wait till winter to see if I won't have to wear scratchy woolen long johns to school.

"Birthday parties and candles are, of course, purely American custom," Papa observed. "But to have many continuing celebrations as you and Zoe have with this year's birthday is how Greeks like to enjoy a feast day. You are setting a new style in holidays."

It seemed the right moment to offer everybody

some *kourabiedes,* and I asked Mama to bring out a plate of them.

"MMMmmm." Ferdie's eyes were rolling and his Adam's apple bobbing as he finished swallowing his *kourabie.* "That has to be one of the best cookies in the world. Where d'you buy these?"

"You can't buy them anywhere. I mean, bakeries here don't make these."

I eyed him as an idea wiggled its way into my head. There was still one whole layer left in my box. And next week I was invited back to Katerina's.

Mama, who was clearing the dirty dishes, smiled and declared, "Zach has given time to Zoe and to the *neife* and, as you can see, it is better to give than to receive."

She was just making conversation, I hoped. But then again, I wondered. Mama has a way of knowing what I'm thinking before I think it.

When she moved into the kitchen and out of hearing, I took my chance.

"Maybe, Ferdie . . . it might cost money, y'understand, but I just might be able to get you some more."

"How many can I get for a nickel?" asked Ferdie eagerly.

My whole face curled up in a big grin. Lucky me. At last I'd found something that I could *sell dear,* just the way the business book said.

4

The Might of Right

Lightning flashed in the night sky just as if someone was pulling a light chain off and on. Thunder rumbled, but nothing came after it.

Georgie, wincing with each flash, asked nervously, "Uh, Zach, maybe we better move off the curb? Go inside, maybe?"

"It's forgotten how to rain, Georgie. We're safe here, anyway," I answered, looking around to double-check that we weren't near any cars or under any wires.

Yesterday's storm had brought down some power lines at George Street and Central Avenue but not much rain and no relief from the heat wave. At least if we stayed outside, I wouldn't have to look at Zoe, whose name oughtta be spelled p-e-s-t.

This afternoon she'd glued herself to my side the way she does so often, and I'd completely forgotten that she was there. Until, that is, we started talking about going swimming. Carlson's Pool costs money, so going there was out of the question. Lansing Pool is still closed, and since the canals are too dirty, there was only one place left: the Mohawk River, the Mighty Mohawk, as the Indians used to say.

That's when Zoe piped up with her, "I'm gonna tell Mama on you. I'm going home right now to tell what you said."

She'd spoken grimly, her black olive eyes wide and scared looking. On account of the Cohoes Falls and the current in the river, some people say it's dangerous to swim there.

Ferdie and Karl—all of us—called her a tattletale and a squealer, but she just hung on to the side of my pants as if she was all set to drag me out of the river. Naturally, we didn't go.

I can't really blame Ferdie and Karl for being mad at me. Here it was the longest heat wave in the history of the U.S., and *my* sister had plugged up our way to cool off.

"If they'd just open the pool . . ." Georgie groaned. "Summer's half gone already."

"Mayor says the city doesn't have any money 'cause some of the mills and people aren't paying their taxes," I reminded him.

"Isn't there enough to pay for the half of summer that's left?" asked Georgie.

"How should I know? It's got something to do with a lawsuit about the city budget. It's all politics, my father says."

In the next lightning flash, I saw Ferdie and

Karl coming up the street. Remembering how we'd parted in the afternoon, I was surprised when they plopped down on the curb next to us. Both started to talk at the same time.

"You guys missed it. . . ." "Didn't you hear the sirens?" "I'll bet he gets it when he gets home. . . ."

When I managed to untangle the story, it turned out that some big kids from Breslin Avenue had gone in skinny-dipping north of Reavy Bridge after it got dark. Coming back across the river, one guy got tired and started going under. And he almost took his two friends with him. But a patrol car going by heard them yelling, and the cops brought them all in safely.

There was silence at the end of the story. We didn't look at one another. I couldn't help wondering if they were remembering, as I was, that last week another kid had had a narrow escape by the Ontario Street bridge.

Clearing my throat, I asked, "Anybody besides me feel some drops? I think it's going to rain for real. See you tomorrow, guys."

Despite the thunder and lightning, Zoe had not awakened. She slept on her stomach, with legs pulled up high under her chest. Her humped-up rump made an inviting target, but I didn't give it a whack. She's not the worst kid in the world. You gotta understand she means well.

I said that to Ferdie and Karl the next morning

when they complained about her tagging along behind us to the Regent Theater. Max, the manager, had promised last week to let all of us in to the movies free if we cleaned up the trash and weeds by the fire exit.

"When he said we could earn a free ticket, he didn't mean Zoe, too," Karl argued. "A little kid like her makes us all look like we're just fooling around, and I won't go to the movies with her."

"Relax, Karl." Lowering my voice, I said, "Zoe doesn't know what we're doing it for, so she doesn't expect anything. We can pretend this is a game and send her home after the 'game' is done."

When I told Zoe we were pioneers clearing the forest to make a homestead, she set herself to pulling up all the little weeds that we were ignoring. In the end, having all that small stuff cleared away made the whole job look neater, more tidy.

"You have lots better games than anybody, Zach. That's why I like to play with you guys more than Monique. What do we do next?" she asked happily.

"Next" I had to get rid of Zoe, so I told her we were going to make Indian costumes to wear. "I'll cross you and you go on ahead to collect as many big brown bags as you can. We'll cut fringe on the open end and holes at the other end for your head and arms. Get your colored pencils out, too, so we can decorate them."

I was *almost* ashamed of myself but not enough to get stuck with her or done out of my ticket. Turns out I was right, though, not to say anything about going to the movies.

When we went to the lobby to collect our tickets, Max wasn't there. A skinny guy with droopy shoulders and a droopy little mustache said Max was on vacation for the next two weeks. He refused absolutely to give us tickets, saying he didn't know but what we had made up the whole story.

"Furthermore, if I catch any of you kids trying to sneak in without paying, I'll turn you over to the cops," he threatened.

Jerk. Nothing but a little jerk puffed up with his own importance. That's what he was, but the fact remained that he was also in charge of the theater. Some grownups who have power love to use it to flatten kids.

"The worst of it is that by the time Max comes back, there'll be more trash and stuff there. We can't prove we did the job unless we do it twice," I said gloomily as we walked along Remsen Street.

Just then Georgie, coming out of Woolworth's at a fast trot, spotted us and yelled to come quick. I wondered if the five-and-ten might be giving something away for free.

"Hey, guess what I heard from Billy Luddy? They're fixing to open up Lansing Pool. He says by tomorrow it'll be ready."

I whistled. This was better even than a free balloon.

"All right! It's about time, too."

"Let's go by and look. Maybe we can find out when exactly they'll let us in," said Ferdie.

In spite of the heat, we covered the ground to the park in no time. Karl, Ferdie and Georgie were whooping and clowning around so much that the worrisome signs I had noticed didn't register on them.

I hated to say it, but I took a deep breath and pointed out, "For a place that's getting ready to open, there's not much action."

Ferdie, stopping dead in his tracks, asked, "What are you trying to tell us, Killjoy?"

"I don't hear anything: no hammering, no voices, no nothing, and I don't see any pickup trucks parked by the bathhouse. That's what," I explained.

The three guys looked at me the way people in that old Greek play must have looked at the messenger who brought the bad news. If looks could kill, I'd be dead.

"They're all . . . they went to lunch, a long lunch," Ferdie said. "C'mon, guys, let's show Gloomy Gus here how wrong he is."

We shortcut across the grass. Fifty yards up over the little knoll brought us right to the pool fence. Noses pressed against the open spaces, we studied the empty pool and bathhouse. The last hope that I might be proven wrong died.

The walk back took forever. Somebody should tell Billy Luddy that it's not only soldiers and defense workers who have to be careful about spreading loose talk and rumors. I know Karl, for one, would have bopped Billy on the head if he'd seen him just then.

Scorching hot as it was, we sat on the curb in front of the shoeshine parlor to rest and argue about what to do next.

Ferdie said, "I'm gonna melt. I'm gonna dissolve in a big puddle. Zach, you're always so full of ideas. How come you don't have any for getting the pool open so we can cool off?"

That's the trouble with being smart. People—teachers, Papa and Mama, and now my friends—never stop expecting things from you, miracles even.

Annoyed, I said, "Too bad President Roosevelt had to go to Chicago to get nominated again. Otherwise, I'm sure he'd keep to his schedule of helping me out twice a month."

"Well, how about asking the mayor, then? He knows you, or anyway, he knows your family now," said Ferdie.

I gave up. I oughtta know by now that Ferdie doesn't understand sarcasm. "Roulier's at the same convention, dummy. Same as Mike Smith.

All the Democrats are. Besides, what good would it do to go ask him? Everybody's already asked over and over to have the pool open and he always answers the same: no money."

"Have a cherry," Ferdie offered, pulling a fistful from his pocket.

I looked at him suspiciously. On our way to the Regent, we had passed by Nasser's Fruit Market. But I hadn't actually seen Ferdie lift anything, so I helped myself to one. It was just sour enough to juice up my dry mouth. We sat there spitting cherry pits into the road, trying to see who could spit the farthest.

I don't know whose cherry pit it was that hit the man's pant leg. Maybe more than one pit landed, because he broke off his conversation with the other fellow and stopped in the middle of crossing the street to look at us. When they had to swerve around the four of us to step up on the curb, both men looked annoyed.

"You can get hurt playing in the street," warned the one with the straw hat, the kind the Elks wear in parades. You could tell he thought we'd been doing something that we shouldn't, but he couldn't quite figure out what.

I recognized him. He's a big shot lawyer, big shot because he heads up the Republicans like Mike Smith does the Democrats.

"Can't you kids find a better place to be?" Without pausing, the man moved to the door of the Remsen Shoeshine Parlor.

I hate that dumb kind of question, the kind where the person asking doesn't really want an answer.

He held open the screen door for his friend and said, "Can't keep the kids off the streets today. You'd think their parents would find a way to keep them busy."

The two disappeared into the dim, awning-shaded store. I thought of how busy we'd been all morning, all for nothing; I thought of our pool closed all summer, and I felt the heat start. It was inside heat, not outside from the sun.

Karl, who must have felt the same way, said angrily, "Yeah, we know a better place to be. Lansing Pool. If this dumb city would just open it."

I exploded. "It's people like them who messed up our summer by not paying taxes, and they're criticizing us? Boy, they have a nerve! Why, they're the whole reason we're out in the street."

"I'd like to see you tell them that. I would. Because it surely is the truth." Karl was nodding his head vigorously in agreement.

"Zach isn't going to tell them off. He wouldn't dare," said Ferdie.

I stood up. "Who says?"

"I say. Even you are not that crazy," Ferdie answered.

"It's not crazy to say what you think when somebody is being unfair," I argued.

Ferdie looked back at the screen door and then up at me. "And just how're you going to do it? Go in, say you want a shoeshine, then tell those men off while you're sitting there?"

"The heat has fried your brains, Ferdie. Have you forgotten that this particular place of business is owned and run by Nick the Greek? A man from the same part of Greece as a certain family named Poulos, a man I call Barba Nico, which is practically like saying Uncle Nick? And that I am welcome to go in there whenever I want for a drink of water, to use the toilet or do anything I feel like doing?" I finished.

At the same time I crossed my fingers, because Barba Nico had never said those exact words to me. Still, it's a fact that Greeks do everything to help one another, so I wasn't really lying.

"Even if you do go in, those guys wouldn't pay any attention to a kid."

Ferdie has this knack for making me mad. In an argument he flip-flops from one side to the other. First he wants a miracle from me, then he says I can't do anything to make a difference.

"Whether they pay attention or not isn't the point. It's the principle of the thing. We have been accused unfairly. I not only dare say so, I *double dare*."

Until that popped out, I hadn't known I felt that way. It gave me a funny feeling to think that I held such ideas in my head without knowing it.

"We-ll?" Ferdie prodded, looking from me to the door and back again.

I stood there like someone who's let too much toothpaste out of the tube and can't get it back in. If those men hadn't been so high and mighty about kids . . . if Ferdie hadn't pushed me . . . .

I swallowed hard. Blaming Ferdie or those men was too easy. The truth of the matter is: I have a big mouth. And now I didn't dare to not take up my own double dare. Leastways, not if I wanted to look any of the guys in the eye after.

So, with my heart playing leapfrog, I marched over to the screen door while Ferdie and Karl drifted over to stand one on each side of the door-way outside.

Sitting up high in chairs the way you do on a shoeshine stand, the two men looked like they were on thrones with Barba Nico at their feet.

"*Nero, parakalo*," I murmured to Barba Nico, who was putting polish on the lawyer's white shoes.

Barba Nico without a word jerked his head toward the back room where he sleeps. So far, so good. Getting a drink of water in his closet kitchen gave me a minute more to think. Calm, cool and collected, that's the way to go about it, I decided over the second drink. Finally, feeling a little sloshy in the stomach, I pushed myself to stroll casually back into the store part.

"*Efharisto,*" I said to Barba Nico. Mama says "please" and "thank you" are the most powerful words, and that if you learn just those two in every language, you can go right around the world without any trouble.

Mr. Big Shot Lawyer didn't seem to have ever heard that. Breaking off the conversation with his friend, he ordered, "Make sure you wipe that front edge of the sole."

Barba Nico shifted the cigar stub in his mouth from the left side to the right without saying anything, not even pointing out that the edge had already been wiped clean. He's a funny kind of Greek: He doesn't talk much.

The lawyer, noticing me, added, "Watch him, kid. You might learn something useful, something that would get you an honest day's work."

That did it.

"I do an honest and *hard* day's work *every* day, mister. Like this morning: I washed sixteen bowls, fourteen plates, thirty cups, and sixty pieces of silverware in my pop's store before going out to clean up enough trash to fill two barrels at the Regent."

I just barely managed to keep myself from shouting. Fortunately, living with Zoe has given me lots of practice in saying things sharply and clearly.

"Speaking of work, mister, since you don't like to see kids out on the street, what are you doing to get them off?" I asked.

"Me?" The lawyer looked startled. "You all aren't my kids. What are you talking about?"

"Talk is cheap. My pop says people oughtta put up and work for what they believe in or shut up. You think kids shouldn't be out on the street, so what's your plan?"

Ignoring his friend, who was saying something about a Lions' Club plan, the lawyer barked, "Listen, you smart-mouth kid, it's the city's responsibility to provide services, not mine."

"Maybe so. But I'll betcha if you and all the other Republicans said you'd pay for a lifeguard at Lansing Pool, the mayor would find money for the other lifeguard in a hurry."

Barba Nico pulled the shine cloth across the toes of the lawyer's shoes with a loud snap. It sounded like a whip cracking.

The lawyer's friend guffawed. He said, "Hey, Will, the kid's made a good case."

Mr. Big Shot didn't seem to think it was so funny. Red-faced, he pulled his feet off the footrests and stood up. Barba Nico, too, stood up, his cigar stub an anchor for the grin that had spread across his face.

Was Mr. Big Shot Lawyer standing up to pay

for his shine? Or getting ready to come after me? I couldn't tell which. Either way, I decided to scram.

Once safe on the other side of the screen door, I fired a last shot back into the store.

"We kids don't pay taxes and we can't vote in a new mayor. No matter what, mister, *you're to blame, not us,* for our sitting on the curbs."

With Ferdie and Karl at my heels and Georgie trailing them, I took off around the corner of Cayuga. Once we were in our alley, we were out of sight to anybody on the street. The four of us flopped breathless on the ground, our backs to the brick wall.

After a minute, Ferdie said, "Gutsy. But what good did that do?"

"Lots. *He* knows that *we* know what's right and who's in the wrong, and I'm not boiling anymore," I said happily.

It was true. I didn't feel nearly so hot, either inside or outside, in spite of having run so hard and fast.

"What if he comes and complains to your pa?" asked Georgie, his voice rising in a squeak. The nuns at his school are always going on about having respect for authority, almost as much as Papa and Mama do.

"He doesn't know who I am, and I don't think he'll find out, either," I answered. Judging from the grin on Barba Nico's face, he'd never tell where I live.

I sat up, straightening my spine as an idea suddenly struck me. If I could stand up so well to somebody as important as that lawyer, why couldn't I do the same and better with a droopy substitute theater manager? Certainly we had right on our side: We'd worked hard and the pay was owed to us.

"Right is might!" I announced. "We all meet at the Regent Theater tomorrow afternoon. By the fire exit where we cleaned up."

"Huh? What are you talking about? What for?" asked Ferdie.

"Y'wanted to see that movie *One Million B.C.,* about the cavemen, didn't you? By hook or by crook, we're going to that show," I declared.

"What time are we goin' to the movies, Zach?"

I groaned out loud.

There was nothing wrong with the question itself. But the direction it came from—the end of the alley—was bad news, and the voice it came in, worse yet. Having Zoe for a sister would make the air go out of anybody's balloon. Her showing up triggered a noisy chorus of hoots and complaints.

"No way will we get in if Zoe's . . . ." "Zach, swear she won't . . . ." "Include me out."

"Tomorrow. I'll take care of her tomorrow," I promised.

"Take care of her" were the exact same words that Papa used the next morning just before he left for Albany again. While Mama watched the store, I was to watch Zoe.

"Zoe's not a baby anymore," I protested. "Do I have to watch her every minute of the day?"

"Well, no, not every minute. Enough to make sure she doesn't need your help," said Papa. "Use your head, Zachary."

He left before I could ask him why we had so much business to do in Albany all of a sudden. But his last words made my life simpler. Using my head, I decided that Zoe could watch herself for *one* afternoon.

When Zoe started mopping the tables after lunch, I made my move. Picking up the broom, I went outside. Zoe could see me sweep off our front steps down to the sidewalk. Once I was out of sight of the doorway, I quick parked the broom in the alley and took off.

I ran the long way to Remsen Street, so Zoe wouldn't catch sight of me doubling back, and I went around the back of the Regent to the fire exit. No point in tipping off the manager ahead of time that we planned to collect on our debt. Once we had a strategy, that was time enough to show up in front.

Holy Toledo! My thoughts scattered like leaves in a windstorm and my feet braked suddenly after

I rounded the corner of the theater. I saw a real mess before me. I don't mean *trash* mess, I mean *people* mess.

Ferdie, Karl and Georgie, like General Custer's army making its last stand, stood shoulder-to-shoulder in a tight half circle. All three wore angry, accusing looks as they faced . . . Zoe Athanasius Poulos!

Zoe, who was crouching next to a bush, had her eyes closed. I could tell she had some muddled, ostrich-like idea that if she couldn't see them, they couldn't see her.

"Where did you come from?" I demanded.

"From home." Zoe's eyes flew open as she answered me. "Soon as I finished my job. A nice lady on Remsen crossed me. I came so you can take care of me like Papa said." Standing up, she gave the guys a look that dared them to try to send her back.

"You sure took care of her, us and any chance we had of getting in," said Karl sourly.

"We can't get in, anyway. That manager's pulled the gate across the lobby and he's unlocking it only after he sells and then punches the ticket," said Georgie.

"Zachary Athanasius Poulos, you tryin' t'*sneak* in?" Zoe asked in a loud, horrified voice. She gave a disapproving "no-no" shake of her head. "That's like stealing. You can't do that."

"See what I mean?" growled Karl. "Shut her up, at least, Zach, so that guy doesn't come out to see what the racket is all about."

The only way ever to shut up Zoe is to answer her questions. I explained about earning the tickets and the manager's refusal to let us in.

"But that's not fair. He's cheating. I want my ticket, too, Zach."

I didn't bother to remind Zoe that, being under six, she herself doesn't need a ticket if she goes in with a paying customer. More important was finding a way to get what was due us.

"C'mon, guys, forget Zoe for now. Let's all concentrate on finding a way to get in. We oughtta have enough brain power to lick that manager. There are four of us and one of him."

Ferdie concentrated so hard that his eyes crossed, while Karl, fixing his eyes on Ferdie's Adam's apple, got a glazed, hypnotized look on his face. Georgie had screwed up his face so tight you'd have thought every tooth in his head ached. I personally couldn't think of anything except how funny they all looked.

I seemed to hear a far-off voice saying, "Zach, open the door. Help! I'm stuck. Open the door, Zach." I shook my head to clear it.

It wasn't my imagination. The soft wail was Zoe's and for real. But where was she? The sense of what she was saying finally soaked in, and I looked over at the fire door of the Regent. A sliver of Zoe still showed outside, the other two thirds of her was inside.

We all rushed over to the door that had pinned her. A wedge on the ground indicated that it must have been propped open a crack, probably to let a little air circulate. I grabbed the edge and pulled open the door wider. Instead of coming out, Zoe moved all the way inside.

Looking back over her shoulder at us, Zoe asked matter-of-factly, "Aren't you guys coming?"

From the darkness, another voice called out, "Get that door shut. It's letting the light in. Somebody tell the manager."

"The cops! That guy will call the cops on us," I hissed. "After her, guys. We gotta get Zoe."

With the fellows crowding after me, I plunged into the theater. *Bang!* The door slammed shut behind us. Instant blackness. I couldn't see my own hand, much less Zoe or anybody else.

A round circle of light shining on the floor moved down the center aisle. The manager was coming to investigate.

"Duck! Scatter," I shouted in a whisper, darting up a side aisle to find an empty seat.

As the flashlight moved across the middle aisle toward the fire door, a wide strip of daylight suddenly showed there again. Of all things, Zoe had managed to open the door by herself. I could just pick her out, back braced against the door, holding it open as she stood facing the theater seats. Huddled in a seat next to two teenagers, I moaned inwardly. We were done for.

"Little girl, what are you doing with that door? Why is that door open?" asked the manager in an angry voice that he didn't bother to lower.

Zoe's voice was equally plain. "To see. It's open to see."

"To see *what?*"

"To see to find my brother. I lost him."

From scared-to-death, I went instantly to rocking with choked-up laughter. Zoe wasn't the first little kid to say those words at the movies. Practically every Saturday, some little kid who's been to the bathroom and can't find where a brother or sister is sitting panics and yells out those words.

"For cryin' out loud, shut the door and leave the kid alone," a man's deep voice called. "We wanna watch the movie, not you two. Any more and we're all gonna ask for our money back."

"Okay, okay," the manager said, lowering his voice and his flashlight. Still suspicious, he muttered, "If I find anybody cheating me, if you're lyin'. . . ."

Bang! The door slammed shut as Zoe moved away from it. Over the grunts of the cavemen on the screen, everybody could hear her say indignantly, "My brother Zach's no cheat 'n' we don't lie. I'm gonna tell my papa what you said."

"Watch out or she'll be suing you for libel, and I'll be a witness. Y'wanna pick on somebody your own size, buddy. I'm over here and ready," the same man taunted. He sounded more than a little mad now.

"Sit down. Sit down anywhere. Don't worry, little girl. You can find your brother when the lights go up," the manager said hastily in a phony, honeyed voice, and the circle of light retreated up the aisle to the back of the theater.

I counted slowly to ten to give Zoe's eyes time to get used to the dark. Then in Greek, which I use in public only for emergencies, I whispered "*Etho,* Zoe . . . *etho*" and waggled my fingers in the air to show her where *etho* was. Good thing Zoe's quick to catch on. In a flash she was up the aisle and into the empty seat on my left. From all different directions, Ferdie, Karl and Georgie, crouching and scuttling like crabs, came and found seats in the row behind.

"Boy, I don't ever want to get into the movies that way again. Once is enough," said Georgie, as we all met again on the corner by Gaudet's Saloon. Coming out of the theater, we had split up, each walking close by a grownup.

Georgie added, "But that was a good show, Zach. I'm glad you planned and got us in."

"Amen. I agree," I said, meaning the "good

100

show" part of what he had said. Technically, if credit was being handed out, Zoe was the one who actually got us into the Regent, but I didn't see any need to point that out.

"Zach, Zach, what's a . . . lie bell?" Zoe asked, tugging at my pants leg to get my attention. "We don't have a lie bell at church, do we?"

I hate to say I'm stumped, especially to Zoe. To gain time, I repeated, "A lie bell? . . . Oh, *libel*." I *did* know the answer to that one. On the radio, George Burns and Gracie Allen had done a show where George was going to sue someone for libel. "Libel, Zoe, is if someone makes untrue insults about you in public and gives you a bad name. You can go to court and make him take it all back."

"C'n we do that? Let's take that bad man at the Regent to . . . ." said Zoe eagerly.

"No, no." While Zoe had told the truth and nothing but the truth at the theater, I didn't need her running around town telling Papa and other people exactly how we'd collected on the promise of free tickets. "You need a lawyer to sue, and anyway, this manager is there for only another week."

Zoe accepted that, but something from our conversation nagged at me all the way through supper. I went back over what we had been talking about. Libel and lawyers. That's what was making me uneasy.

Pointing a finger at a lawyer, I decided, could

be a risky business. I tried to recall just what I had said to the lawyer the day before. Besides blaming him, had I called him any insulting names? I couldn't remember.

"Such a frown, *Zaharia*. Is that any way to greet your father, who's been away all day?" Papa's voice interrupted my thoughts. He nodded to Mama, saying, "Yes. The business in Albany is all settled."

I hadn't even seen him come in. I pasted a smile onto my face as I wondered if he knew whether a kid under eighteen could be sued.

"I see you brought home lots of news for Mama," I said, spying the bundle of Greek newspapers under his arm.

"Yes, and some news of interest for you, too, Zach. I got off the bus at Remsen Street and saw Barba Nico."

I could feel my face burning, and I tried to change the subject. "Does the paper say it's gonna rain? Is the heat wave going to break?"

My luck had run out. Papa continued as if I hadn't said a word.

"Barba Nico tells me your tongue was on wheels yesterday. It ran faster than a train, I hear."

"I didn't start it, Papa. He practically called us kids lazy bums. Ask Barba Nico. He'll tell . . . ." I said heatedly.

"Relax, boy. Barba Nico did tell me. To attack *hypocrisia* is not a bad thing."

"Is that the lawyer's name? But I didn't attack him, Papa. I . . . ."

To my surprise, Papa laughed. "No, no. *Hypocrisia* is the Greek word that means pretending to all kinds of virtues. Saying one thing, but doing the other. The English word is the same as in the Greek. A person who behaves that way is a *hypocrite*."

Talk about dumb! I felt younger and stupider than Zoe for misunderstanding. Then I realized what Papa had said. He *agreed* that I had done the right thing.

"That wasn't all I heard," Papa added. "Today that lawyer told Barba Nico it's not yet official, but you may see the pool open by August first. Lions, Republicans, the Rotary Club all met this morning with the mayor to say they going to pay half the money it costs to keep the pool open. The mayor, he says okay, the Democrats pay the other half to keep the bathhouse clean."

Wowie! I couldn't wait to tell the kids. Thanks to Papa, I'd be scooping even the *Cohoes American*. And, thanks to him, I had this great new word. How did he say it? Hippo-crit. I could find lots of uses for that one.

5
The Big Move

I would be lying if I didn't say that as each hour ticked off, I was less and less sure of how I felt. I would be lying, too, if I didn't say that deep down I wished five o'clock would hurry up and come. Even though once we were on that bus, I probably might never see Ferdie, Karl or Georgie again. Anything would be better than this swampy no-man's land of being here in Cohoes but belonging already in Albany. I'd been feeling that way ever since Papa broke the news.

"Who do you figure is gonna be the first one in the water when the pool opens tomorrow? Karl's legs are longer, but Zach moves faster. Anybody wanna make a bet?" asked Georgie.

"I pick Zach, and if I win, I get to be first in Follow the Leader down the sliding board," said Ferdie, quickly staking his claim.

"You lose, Ferdie," I said. "Remember, I won't be here tomorrow."

Ferdie's face was almost comical to see as he realized what he'd done. Now that it was so close to time to say good-by, everybody was kind of tiptoeing around to avoid the subject. We all were being a little more careful of what we said, a little more polite, like people on a bus who talk but get off at different stops.

Ferdie stared at the alley wall behind me and said, "Gee, Zach, I'm sorry. . . . I mean, we'll write and tell you how it was."

Funny. A month ago I had worried night and day about the possibility of having to leave the Miss Liberty. Now, when it's happening for real—we are truly moving—I wish I was already there. I can't wait to see the new restaurant, to find out what the new neighborhood looks like. The difference, I suppose, is that nobody's *making* us move. We *chose* to do it ourselves.

That's what Papa's trips to Albany were about. He was making a deal to buy Mustaki's restaurant. The new restaurant is all furnished, Papa says. So he sold the tables, the chairs—everything movable in the Miss Liberty—and used that money to seal the bargain. We're going to pay the rest of the price little by little each month.

"Remember, Zach, how you worked on Georgie to go off the big board last year? Well, I'll see that he does it this year for sure," said Karl, giving Georgie a little shove in advance.

"I have a plan," said Ferdie.

I tried not to snort at the thought of Ferdie planning something.

"See, if we take sandwiches tomorrow, we won't have to come home until they kick us out at closing time."

Karl nodded at Ferdie and said, "Good thinking. Want to meet on the corner?"

Georgie, looking up at Ferdie, asked, "What time do we meet?"

Ferdie always has had ambitions to step into my shoes. I knew that. Well, I wasn't on the bus for Albany yet.

Interrupting, I said, "Speaking of time, there's just enough left. Who's coming with me up to the convent yard?"

"*Now?* You want to make a raid there *now?*" an incredulous Ferdie asked.

"The priest or some nun will catch you," said Georgie flatly.

"And you'll miss the bus," Karl, frowning, added.

I had everybody's attention, and I dealt with the last remark first. "There's plenty of time, and the nuns usually go away in August, remember? I thought we'd pick up some pears for Zoe and me, a last souvenir, like. You guys came with me when I took that bone to Yankee and said good-by to him, so I figured you'd want to come along on this trip, too. Of course, if you're chicken, Zoe and I'll go alone."

They all looked at me and at Zoe and then looked

uneasily at one another. Always before, we've gone when everybody up at the convent was pretty sure to be busy praying in church, and always I'd left Zoe home. Even then, we'd had a close call or two.

But there was no arguing the fact that Zoe had to come with us. There was no "home" here for her to stay at. Our beds and stuff had been loaded first thing this morning into Mr. Pappas's truck, and Mama had gone with the men to boss the setting up in the new house. Zoe and I were to follow on the five o'clock bus after saying our good-bys to everybody.

And nobody could argue much more about getting caught. That would be as good as admitting he was scared.

I added, "Tomorrow, after your dry sandwiches, you'll want something juicy, won't you?"

Tying it up with what they were planning clinched it.

It's a steep climb up from the tow path and the canal, but most of it's through shady green sumac and skinny birches. On top we stopped at the fence to catch our breaths and check out the fat, old pear tree in the convent yard. The pears nearest the fence always ripen first, which means they'd already been picked over by both nuns and kids. We'd have to go farther in, closer to the convent house.

"Remember, guys, stay out of the line of sight

from the windows. Zoe, you stick with me. What we want is a lightning strike."

Scraping through the opening where the fence had broken down, feeling the excitement in slipping from tree trunk to tree trunk, finding a good branch to pull myself up by, and jamming hard green pears into pockets, hoping we wouldn't get caught, I felt a sharp pang like someone tightened a string around my heart. The memory of this trip would have to last me a long time. Who knows if I'd find anything like this in a big city like Albany?

"Pssst. Somebody's at the window. I think the door's opening." Georgie's hoarse whisper cut into my thoughts.

Faster than a speeding bullet, as they say in the comics, I was at the fence break. Then I remembered Zoe. Wheeling around, I saw her still bent double, searching the grass for a perfect pear.

"For cryin' out loud!" In my exasperation, I forgot to whisper. "C'mon. *Now,* Zoe Athanasius Poulos, or I won't let you move to Albany with us."

A black-robed figure stood motionless in the back doorway of the convent. Between my shout and Zoe's white underpants showing as she bent over, whoever had come out couldn't possibly miss us. But the figure didn't move.

Fortunately, Zoe did. Move, that is. Her feet came unstuck and she flew across the grass. I boosted her up and through the fence. Just before we plunged down the side of the hill, I took a last look back. I had guessed right. Like a black bird with wings flapping, the watcher finally had stepped out to make shooing gestures and shout. I smiled to myself.

All the way to city hall where the bus leaves from, we laughed and pounded one another on the back. Maybe we should have shook hands or something like that to say good-by. That's how my friend Josh Braga, the only black man in Cohoes, had said good-by to me when he'd left for a big new job in New York City. But I felt foolish doing that with Ferdie, Karl and Georgie, so I just pushed Zoe up the bus steps, telling her to find a seat by a window, and over my shoulder, I said, "Be seein' ya, guys."

Sitting down next to Zoe, I checked my pockets for the slip of paper with directions on where to go after we got off the bus. Between the pears, my yo-yo, jackknife and money, it took a while to locate it. Omigosh. I'd almost forgotten the last important thing I had to do before leaving. Telling the driver I had to get off for a minute, and with a "Sure" from him, I swung back down the steps.

"Here, Ferdie. I want you to keep this. A souvenir, so you don't forget me till we get together again," I said, shoving my gift into his pocket.

As the bus pulled away, my last sight of Ferdie was of him looking dumbfounded at the coin that he'd brought up out of his pocket.

"Why's Ferdie look so surprised? What did you give him?" Zoe asked.

"I gave him a present, something to remember me by."

"Oh, for good-by, like I gave Monique my nighttime diamonds?" she asked. Zoe had spent most of last night collecting the "diamonds"—that's what she calls fireflies—in a jelly jar to give Monique.

"Sort of."

The round, shiny, coin-like token that I gave Ferdie had been given to me by a customer as a tip. One side says A SAMPLE OF ALUMINUM IN THE NEW UNION PACIFIC TRAIN BUILT BY THE PULLMAN CAR CO. and it has the date, 1934, so it's already getting to be old and valuable. On the other side, right under the picture of a streamlined locomotive, it says LUCKY PIECE.

I'm plenty lucky already, what with moving to the capital of New York State. And if Ferdie never noticed that the nuns and priest always wait till our pockets are filled before they chase us away, he *needs* a lucky piece.

The bus was passing Cohoes High School on our left, and I realized suddenly that I would never go to school there. Maybe Karl and Ferdie are kind of lucky, at that. They *know* where they'll be going to school in a few weeks and even where they'll go to high school. Whereas I don't know yet the name—or maybe it's a number—of my new school or how to find the street it's on, much less which high school I'll end up at. Albany has more than one.

I wished my stomach would sit still. The sight of Zoe bouncing around in her seat like a Mexican jumping bean was not helping any. She wrestled a brown bag out of the big patch pocket on her dress and started pulling stuff out of the bag.

"Mama said I should bring just one on the trip, but I couldn't make up my mind which one. So finally I made a choice and bringed both," she said, pointing happily to the box of colored pencils and the embroidery stuff that Papa and Mama had given her as a birthday present.

On her lap she spread out the guest towel with a flower design that she was stitching and placed the bright-colored embroidery thread on top in curving loops. Then she insisted that I admire her baby rainbow. But the ride was too jerky for her to thread the needle or stitch and she hadn't brought any paper to color, so she stuffed everything away again.

"Zach, do we gotta cross the river on this bus, too?" Zoe asked, kneeling on her seat to see out the window better.

"I think we stay on this side of the river."

" 'N' when we go to Greek school in Albany, we don't hafta cross any rivers?" Zoe looked at me, her face puckered by an anxious frown.

"I don't think there are any rivers in the middle of the city," I answered cautiously. "Why are you so worried about rivers, Zoe?"

"Not rivers, bridges. Y'know you told me how that one opens up to let the boats go through? Every time we crossed, I prayed hard, so we never fell through," she explained with a shiver. "I wish God had a telephone. I'd feel more sure about praying if I could talk to him that way."

For once Zoe had captured every bit of my attention. She was talking about the short, humped-up bridge between Cohoes and Troy that our bus went over when we went to Greek school. It swings apart for big boats coming up from the Hudson River.

"Do you mean every single time we crossed, you thought the bridge was going to open up while we were on it? And that we were going to fall through and drown in the Mohawk?" I asked, watching her head bob up and down in "Yes."

I was about to laugh, when a picture popped suddenly into my head. I saw myself a few years back zigzagging to avoid the cracks in the sidewalk after I'd heard that rhyme. The one that goes: Step on a crack, break your mother's back.

"Next time you're worried, Zoe, *ask me*. The bridge *can't* open, not until the guard gates are down at each end. Anyway, Albany has its own

Greek school, so you don't have to worry anymore about crossing into Troy."

"Good. I wanna live there," she declared.

I put my arm around Zoe's shoulders, gave her a little squeeze and turned her again to face the window. "Watch the scenery now. You can pretend you're Christopher Columbus, 'cause you've never been this way before."

Neither had I, as a matter of fact. It made me a little nervous, and I hoped the bus driver wouldn't forget to let us off at the stop that I'd told him.

"Zach?"

I was too busy trying to spot some signs to answer her. Papa had said the trip should take about an hour, but without a watch I couldn't tell how far along the way we were.

"Zachary Athanasius Poulos. I need to know."

I sighed. When Zoe uses my full name, it means she's not going to let go or give up until she gets what she wants.

"Zach, I need to know: How do you make friends? I mean, how does it work? I don't remember if I know how to do it. And where am I going to find them?"

I swear I'll be dead in my grave and Zoe will climb down into the hole to ask me one more impossible question. How do *I* know where she's going to find friends?

"Well, Zoe, you'll . . . ." I stopped. Come to think of it, I have no memory of ever "making" friends. I mean, my friends have always been there. I can't recall when or how I first met any of the kids on our block.

Nobody could take Ferdie's place, or Karl's or Georgie's, either, for that matter. They would always be my first, best friends. But would there be any kids my age . . . or any kids at all on the block where we were going? What if they were all big kids? The kind that like to boss around other smaller kids like . . . like me. Or what if they were the kind who pick fights with anybody who isn't just like them?

To tell the truth, I fight better with words than with my fists. I shifted in my seat and wished my stomach would stop bopping around like a butterfly in a flower bed.

"Zach, I'm . . . shy, ain't I?"

Someone had once said that in her hearing. "Shy? You? Never!" I said. If there is only one thing in the world that I am positive of, it's that Zoe doesn't have a shy bone or a drop of shyness in her body. I added, "Stop stewing. You'll have more friends than a dog has fleas. Even if there aren't any kids where we live, you'll find lots in school."

If that was true enough to tell Zoe, it ought to be true for me, too. I made up my mind to stop worrying about bridges that we didn't have to cross.

"Look at all the grass and the big houses, Zoe," I said, pointing out the window.

"People here must be rich," exclaimed Zoe.

"Maybe."

A sign said we were going through Loudonville. The houses, few and far between, had enough grass around each to make a small park. Even so, I didn't think I'd want to live in a place like this. There were no movies or stores to walk to and no sidewalks to play stoop ball or hopscotch. I didn't see any horses or barns, either. It wasn't real country and it wasn't real city. Thanks, but no, thanks, I said to myself, just before we came to the sign that said ENTERING CITY OF ALBANY.

The houses came closer together and the streets reminded me of Cohoes, and suddenly we were on a viaduct. Way below us was a spaghetti of railroad tracks in a ravine. Coming off the viaduct, I saw a big, red brick building stretching out around a half circle of grass. A school or public building of some kind? Maybe the Capitol, the building where the governor of New York State sits and works?

"Northern Boulevard."

I wish I had somebody I could ask questions of all the time the way Zoe has.

"Northern Boulevard," the bus driver called out again. "It's your stop, kids."

"Your bag, Zoe. Have you got your bag?" I asked, patting my own pockets to make sure I had the phone number to call in an emergency plus two nickels to make calls. We scrambled hastily out of our seats and down the aisle.

"Central Avenue is a few blocks over," the driver said just before he closed the door.

Clinton Avenue to Orange Street. That's one block. I counted it off mentally and tried to wiggle my fingers. Zoe was clutching my hand so tightly the blood had stopped circulating.

Orange to Sheridan Avenue. Yep, here was another viaduct. Boy, Albany must be built on more hills than the city of Rome. My directions said this one ended at Central Avenue where the new store was.

"Does this bridge come apart, Zach?" a worried Zoe asked, halting at the corner.

"No, no. This is a viaduct. Viaducts go over a piece of low land or over other roads. They save you the trouble of having to go down one side and climbing back up the other to get across a gully." We were so close now. I was impatient to get there. "Let's get a move on."

But before she would step on that viaduct, Zoe made me cross my heart that it never, never opens. Since the viaduct sloped up, at the halfway point we were more than a couple of stories above the streets below. When I leaned over the railing to look down, I felt like somebody in an airplane.

Tires squealing to a sudden stop cut into my imaginings, and, looking ahead, I whistled softly. Two cars from opposite directions on Central Avenue had tried to turn at the same time onto the viaduct. They had stopped just an inch short of a crash. The two cars were so angled that neither one could move forward without denting the other, and so far, neither one was backing off to allow the other to move ahead.

Like everyone else walking on the viaduct, Zoe and I put on speed to get to the scene of the near accident. Already cars were starting to pile up in every direction on both Central Avenue and the viaduct. It was turning into a wonderful mess that the two drivers ignored completely as they yelled at one another.

People in the crowd, taking sides, rooted for one driver or the other and shouted advice. Finally a policeman showed up and pulled the two cars and drivers apart. Then the cop waved his billy club at everybody and told them to move along.

The scattering crowd pushed me back against the corner building. Waiting for an opening, I said, "Didn't I tell you, Zoe, that the city has something going on all the time?"

"Zoe, we have to move. . . ." I looked around to take Zoe's hand in mine again.

No Zoe. Not at my side and not anywhere I

looked. I couldn't believe it. The one time in my life when watching Zoe was truly important, and she had slipped out of sight somehow. The crowd had come between us. Maybe if I stepped out to the curb and stood still, she could more easily find her way to my side.

Had I told her the number of the new house? Would she remember the name of the street? I stood very still on the curb for what seemed like a hundred years. Any second now, I told myself, she'd . . . ."

"Hey, boy, you're going to turn into a statue if you stand there much longer," a man crossing the street said.

He was right. I had to make a move of some kind. Looking left and down the block where the store and apartment were located, I didn't see any Zoe. The block to my right was longer, more crowded, and I couldn't see very far down it. I *had* to make a move.

Praying that I wouldn't get myself lost, too, I stepped off the curb to cross the street. My eyes had kind of filled up. I didn't want anyone to see them that way, so I kept my head bowed as I started down the long block. The flash of pink on the gray sidewalk showed up plainly enough, but my brain didn't register the meaning of it until I'd gone two stores beyond.

When it did sink in, I backed up so fast that I

knocked a lady's bag out of her hand. Sweating hard, I apologized and bent over to pick up the long pink loop. I wasn't mistaken. Who else but Zoe could have dropped that hank of pink embroidery thread? She *had* gone this way, she must have.

Dodging from side to side like someone in a crazy game of hopscotch, I raced up the avenue, trying to see between and around the people walking. No sign of Zoe's sun-bright dress. I slowed down. This avenue was big, a main drag solid with businesses and lots of traffic. I couldn't believe she'd try to cross it, but I looked across the street, too. No Zoe anywhere. Little streams of icy sweat trickled from my armpits down my sides.

I went back to walking slowly with my head down because I could think of nothing else to do. A long string of black thread might have fallen from someone's pants, but the fact that I found it in front of a toy store window gave me hope again.

At the end of the block I couldn't tell which way to go. Straight ahead, or right onto Lexington? I scanned the sidewalk for another clue.

"If you're hunting for gold, kid, I picked it all up," said a man's voice. He stood in the doorway of the drugstore, grinning and picking his teeth with a toothpick.

"My sister. She's really small for her age, with short black hair and a yellow dress?" My voice rose into a question as I hoped against hope that he'd been in the doorway when she went past.

A small miracle happened. His face sobered, and he nodded.

"Check by the Woolworth's in the next block. She should be about there by now. She looked too little to be by herself. But she wouldn't answer or talk to me, just kept right on going."

"Mama told her never to talk to strangers or take a ride with one. Thanks, mister." I sprinted across the street with new hope.

"Zach, Zach." I heard her voice calling before I got as far as the five-and-ten, and I gave God a quick "thank-you," promising Him a longer one later. But I still didn't see anything yellow up ahead. Navy blue uniformed legs suddenly blocked my view. Cop or no cop, this was no time to stop. I moved sideways to get around him.

"Well, now, sonny. You on your way to a fire? What's your hurry?" he asked, blocking my way again.

I raised my eyes to answer and exclaimed, "I . . . I . . . Holy Toledo, Zoe!"

Draped down the front of the policeman's uniform like some fancy scarf were Zoe's stick-skinny legs with her good white socks and patent leather shoes. She sat on the policeman's shoulders, her chin resting on his cap and her arms wrapped around his head to keep from falling off. The signs

of crying—smudged cheeks and red-tipped nose—
were as plain as day.

"Who told you to go up *there*?"

"I told her, sonny. So she could look for the big
brother who's supposed to be taking care of her,"
said the policeman in a don't-argue-with-me voice.

"Why'd you get lost, Zach?" asked Zoe.

What a question. But I didn't dare yell at her
in front of the cop. After I convinced him that I
knew where we had to go, he bent down and let
Zoe off.

"Stay on this side of the street. Number seven
should be in the first block of Central, across from
the little park," he told us.

We covered the block in between on the double.
I yanked Zoe past the toy store without letting her
stop to look at the windows. It seemed like the
least I could do in the way of punishment.

Number seven was three stories high with a
drugstore on the first floor. Our flat was on the top
floor, but no lights shone in the front windows.
Papa and Mama were probably working in the
kitchen. The street door closing behind us cut the
light in the hall, and it got dimmer yet as we
climbed the second flight. At the top, a little daylight came from the uncurtained windowpanes in
a door.

Hurrying now to get out of the dark, silent hall,

I turned the knob on the door. Locked. The door was locked, and the room, with our kitchen table piled high with boxes, empty of people. Maybe Papa and Mama were setting up beds somewhere. Zoe started to whimper. I banged loudly on the door, calling to get Mama and Papa's attention. Nobody came.

"Oh, Zach, they got lost, too. We're never gonna see them again," said Zoe, and she burst into noisy tears.

"Ss-ssh. I can't hear if they're coming."

But shushing Zoe was a waste of time because (a) nobody could shut her up, and (b) there was nothing to hear. Panic emptied my head. I wanted to lie down on the floor and close my eyes until a new day came when we could make a better beginning.

"Mama can't . . . hic . . . give me my supper . . . hic . . . an' I'm hungry. Oh, Zach, are we gonna . . . hic . . . die?" asked Zoe, sobbing, talking and hiccuping all at the same time.

I straightened up from the door where I'd been leaning and said firmly, "Don't be silly. We've got pears to eat, so you can't die of starvation, anyway."

The mention of food put my brain back in working gear. Food means meals, meals mean restaurant. And we own a new restaurant at Number

11½ Central Avenue. That's where we had to go. Grabbing Zoe's hand, I headed back down the stairs and out the door.

Eleven and a half is a funny number for an address, but I wasn't smiling. In fact, I was frowning as I tried to figure out why I hadn't seen the place on our way down. It had to be on this side of the street since the opposite side was a wedge-shaped little park with a horse watering trough at the pointy end. I have an excellent memory, if I do say so myself, so I went mentally back up the block.

Next to the drugstore, a newsroom, then a big new car showroom. After that . . . a closed-up, padlocked place and a . . . tailor, I think. Why didn't I remember a restaurant anywhere in there?

Never mind. All I had to do was to count the doors from Number 7 on. A beaut of a Plymouth sat on the floor of the Armory Garage, which I realized suddenly had to be Number 11 by my count.

So 11½ was . . . *this*? No wonder I couldn't bring up a picture of it in my mind's eye. If you blinked as you walked past, you'd miss seeing it. That's how big the place was.

A metal Coca-Cola sign covered the lower half of the front. The upper part was a window that opened by swinging up from the bottom, and all the rest of the front was painted bright orange. A narrow shelf stuck out from just below the window, so a person could collect his order without going inside. The bill of fare glued to the back of the cash register bore out my suspicions. What we were looking at was not a real restaurant; it was a crummy *hot dog stand.*

"Ma-mmaa! Mama, *eirthame . . . eirthame.*"

Zoe's shrieks as she spotted Mama and Papa through the screen door cut into my numb shock. Trust Zoe to yell at the top of her lungs that we had arrived when everybody could see that we had. Instantly, she had the screen door open and was running into Mama's welcoming arms. I took my time following.

Inside, the place seemed about as wide as a bus. A small counter, half a dozen stools, and a single table against the partition that screened a kitchen—that was the whole store. Papa, wearing his white apron, stood behind the counter with Mustaki, the man who had sold us this little crackerbox.

"So, Odysseus has arrived safely with his crew," said Papa with a smile. He was talking about the Greek hero who had wandered for ten years before getting home from the Trojan War.

I tried a smile. It came out slightly lopsided, the way a phony one always does. Just then, Mama swept me up with a big hug and kisses on both cheeks. That smothered the smile, thank heavens.

"I got all turned around," Zoe announced

125

proudly, as if it were something to her credit.

"*Po-po-po,*" said Mama, making the Greek sounds for sympathy and looking alarmed as Zoe told about the lady who by mistake helped her to cross the street. Mama shook her head and added, "So lucky you were. We hear too many stories about people kidnapping children."

"Never, Mama. Any kidnapper who talked to Zoe for even a minute would give her right back. He'd never keep her," I said.

Ignoring Zoe, who stuck her tongue out at me, I gave *my* version of the day. It took a long time to tell because of all the interruptions. Mustaki kept calling Papa every other minute to be introduced and wait on still another customer. A lot of those customers must be what we call "regulars," because he knew them by name.

Each time Mustaki delivered the same speech. "This here is Athanasius Poulos, the new owner. Call him Pop. He's gonna be workin' hard for you. Me, I go take it easy in Greece."

Mama told me that, really, he's going over there to bring his family back to America because he's so worried about the war in Europe.

For supper, we all had hot dogs at the single table. My milk was good and cold on account of this dump had a shiny new electric refrigerator. (In the Miss Liberty, we only had a wooden icebox, and sometimes the milk turned sour before we

126

could sell it.) I have to admit, too, that the chocolate cream pie we had for dessert was one of the best I ever tasted.

"Well, Zach, what do you think of our new place?" Papa asked as he came back to the table from waiting on another customer.

How could he ask? Coming from the Miss Liberty with eight tables and twelve stools to this nameless, junky looking little place, what could I say? I used to think Papa was a smart man. How could he have agreed to spend all our money on this bad joke of a store?

"Okay, I guess," was the best I could manage. He looked so happy, I didn't want to hurt his feelings.

"Okay only?" Papa's one eyebrow quirked up the way it does when he's amused. Turning to Mustaki, he said, "You're right. The location is superb. I just checked the tally on the cash register. With five hours still to closing time, I have rung up already twice what I did in a day at the Miss Liberty."

"Listen and learn, *Zaharia*," he said, turning back to me. "Big is not necessarily better. For a business, location is everything."

"They are falling over from tiredness and you're trying to give him business lessons? Stop," said Mama.

Actually, Papa's words had brought me wide

awake. *Twice as much as what we made in the Miss Liberty?* I thought about all the steady customers, and about all the traffic on the avenue. I thought about the new modern refrigerator. It wasn't New Year's Day but I made a resolution, anyway: no more judging on first impressions.

"Better you and Mustaki should show me where everything is kept, so I can help tomorrow with the breakfast rush," Mama told Papa. Turning back to me, she asked, "If I give you the key, can you take Zoe back and put her to bed by yourself? You won't be scared, will you?"

"You're talking to the bravest boy in Albany County, the one who made such a perilous journey. Shame," said Papa in a mock scolding.

Zoe, who had taken my hand, hugged it hard to her cheek. "My Zach is the bestest, the bravest brother. He doesn't get scared even by bridges and he doesn't stay lost too long. He's the smartest person in the whole world." Sleepily, she repeated, "Bravest brother."

Bravest brother, yes. Anybody who lives with Zoe would win that one. But not the smartest person in the world. I get my looks from Papa. Maybe I should hope that I get some of his brains, too.

Leading Zoe to the door, I told Papa, "We're on our way."

6

All for One

"I'm going out. Just around the corner," I announced as I cleared my dinner plate from the only table in the hot dog stand.

"There now. Didn't I say you would find new friends quickly?" said Mama with a satisfied smile. "And that Tom Thomas has a sister who should be company for Zoe."

I didn't say anything to correct her impression that I was going out to find Tom Thomas. Mama is okay, sort of, for a mother. I mean, she never yells at us in public or in front of other kids, but there are some things she just does not understand.

This Thomas kid and his mother—they're Greek and from the same village as our family—had stopped in today to welcome us to Albany. Because he's just a year older than I, Mama seems to think that automatically makes us friends. I may not be too clear on how you "make friends," but I know that's *not* the way.

The "around the corner" that I planned to go to was a big park, one I've been itching to explore. Across from us, the little park with trees has some benches, a walk down the middle and a couple of war memorials. But a customer told me that Washington Park at the end of Northern Boulevard has the works: flowers, fountains, playground—everything.

"Can I bring my dolly with us?" asked Zoe.

Thinking quickly, I said, "No. And not you, either, Zoe. Where I'm going might be too long a walk, too far, and there might be . . . ."

"And there might be bears and wolves along the way," said Mama dryly. "Come, Zach, enough of your foolishness. You know Zoe cannot go out by herself until she knows the streets and blocks. You *will* take her with you, so she can learn her way around here."

"Mama, do I have to?"

"Zach, do you wish to go out or no? I've told you the conditions."

You can move the Rock of Gibraltar more easily than Mama once she's decided. I made Zoe walk three feet behind me after we'd crossed Central Avenue. Finding the park was simple. Even from two blocks away, I could see a big monument with little flower beds on either side.

"What's it for, Zach? Is this why we came this

way?" asked Zoe, who had caught up with me by the entrance.

"It's a memorial to soldiers and sailors. And no. What we came for is over there," I answered, waving to my right, where I'd spotted the top part of a slide. Because the playground was in a hollow, we couldn't see or hear any kids playing.

Cutting across the grass, we found out the real reason it was so quiet. Swings, volleyball nets, all the equipment was locked up in the shed for the evening. It beats me why people run a playground like an office, from nine to five. Kids don't stop playing after supper; they don't stop until they have to go to bed.

I found out another thing, too. A playground—even with the longest slide I'd ever seen—can be boring. A lot of the fun in a sliding board comes from racing against friends to see who gets the most runs in, or trying to go down in a way that's crazier than the last kid. I mean, how long can a person stand at the bottom catching another person? You need *people* in a playground, and Zoe yelling "Wait for me" and "Catch me, Zach, catch me" doesn't count.

"C'mon. We might as well go back to the main path. We can sniff the flowers or sit on a bench like grownups," I said, feeling cross, and I took off with Zoe at my heels again.

"I want to go buttercupping, Zach."

"Uh-uh. The sign said picking flowers is not allowed. That probably means dandelions and buttercups, too."

"I still like this park, even so," Zoe decided. "It smells good and it makes me feel good."

Privately, I agreed with her. In the dusk the scene reminded me of a painting I saw once on a calendar and liked a lot: little blobs of color that were flower beds, bits of white—statues?—showing through green-leaved trees, and in the distance blurry shapes of people strolling on a path as wide as a street. Out loud, I only said, "Don't go off by yourself."

The people on the benches that lined the path were feeding the pigeons and having polite conversations. Every now and then, like an exclamation mark, an excited voice somewhere ahead cut into that low hum of talk.

Zoe's own voice rose sharply. "I hear kids, Zach. Let's find 'em. Hey, what's that green thing?"

"Zoe, there's lots of green in a park. What are you talking about?"

Following her pointing finger, I looked ahead. Off the path to the right, I saw a green open-frame shape and lots of bobbing heads. "Step on the gas, kid, and we'll see." I tugged Zoe to go faster.

Fenced off by green railings the size of railroad ties, there stood a row of huge wooden chair swings, something like the kind that people have on their front porches or in their backyards. The big ones on either end with two bench seats facing one another could hold four people, even six in a squeeze, while the middle ones in the row carried only two people back to back. Every one of the swings was full.

Zoe and I lined up at the railing behind the people already waiting, and I listened hard to the talk around us to get the lay of the land. It seems people shared swings even if they didn't know one another. The swings got padlocked shut at eight o'clock, so we didn't have much time left to get on.

A girl in front of Zoe turned to ask, "You can't reach to pump, little girl. Have you got anybody to go on with?"

"My big brother, Zach," Zoe answered.

"Jack?" The girl, who was about my age, looked over at me questioningly as if to ask whether she'd got it right. She had hair dark like cherry wood, and eyes so blue they reminded me of the flame on a gas stove.

But I'm not so hard up yet for friends that I have to start looking to girls for company. Ignoring her, I told Zoe to grab a swing if our turn came, while I went to get a drink from the water fountain.

Coming back, I heard Zoe's voice plainly over the creaking of the moving swings. "No fair. It's our swing. Wait till my brother comes."

A girl's voice said, "You guys got off already, now you stay off."

Like an angry cat with a kitten at its side, the dark-haired girl stood with Zoe by a four-seater swing, her one hand on the wooden arm, claiming it. Facing them on the other side of the swing, three boys were yapping away.

"We changed our minds. You can't fill the swing, anyway, with just two of you. . . ." One voice taunted, "Not two. One and a half." "Whatta y'mean? A dumb Mick like her doesn't even count as one," said another jeering voice.

"Hah! I'd rather be a Mick than a moron like you," the girl answered instantly.

Clearly, we had the right to the swing, and as the British general said last week about the Battle of Britain, the best defense is an offense.

"Up you go, Zoe," I said, hoisting her onto the platform of the swing.

Zoe, catching on to my tactics, scrambled under the safety bar into the seat. The other girl was no slouch, either. She hopped on quickly to sit next to Zoe, and I followed, taking the opposite bench seat. Three of us already in the seats should make it harder for them to take it back.

"Regulations prohibit monopolization of the swings by any one person or parties," I said, loudly quoting the rules posted on the side of the frame where we had waited.

I tried to watch the boys without seeming to. Sooner or later, these kids had to make a move. Neither Zoe nor the girl on our side would be much help in a real fight. Well, if worse came to worst, we could start pumping to try and shake them off.

When the thump came of someone jumping on, it was from my left side where I didn't expect it. The swing poles rattled noisily as someone grabbed them.

"Pump," a voice like Donald Duck commanded.

Too startled to obey, I swiveled to look at the stranger who'd joined us. A real runt, he had such thick, springy, black curly hair that his head looked too big for his body. His ears stuck out like propellers, and his nose wouldn't have been out of place on a camel.

In that Donald Duck-like voice, he said to the gang on the other side of the swing, "And with respect to calling people a 'dumb Mick,' Joey Tibbit, you should know that *dumb* by dictionary definition means 'bereft of the power of speech.' You can't honestly say that you've ever seen Patty Aylward without the power of speech, can you?" He continued, "If, in fact, you mean to call her stupid, you should recall that she's one year ahead of grade level. So you're wrong on all counts."

On top of his funny looks and voice, he had an odd way of sounding out every syllable of every word. He said all his "ings," too. Actually, he spoke like somebody who's used to being listened to.

The best that the Joey kid could come back with was, "Oh, I'll bet you all swim like a rock. Why don't you show us by jumping in the lake?"

I knew I could handle this one. Raising my eyebrows and looking down my nose, I said, "Swimming is anti-evolutionary. That's where man is supposed to have had his origins. Why would anyone want to go back to the water?"

The funny-looking kid gave me a look of approval while the enemy side was still trying to sort that out. I thought they might be about to quit and leave us alone when Patty Aylward opened her mouth.

"We'd let you on, Joey-Josephine, but there are already two girls on this swing, and it might be too rough a ride for you." Her voice dripped with sweetness.

We'd have to pay for that one, I could tell. But it was worth it. Clocking this Joey's expression, I could read disbelief and rage traveling around his face. I'd like to have seen tears, too, but you can't have everything. I braced my feet so I could go either way: pump hard or jump off.

"Closing time now. Come back tomorrow," a man's hoarse voice called from the end of the swings. The park attendant held a long pole ready to thread through the frame and lock the swings in place. "All off."

Suddenly my back felt very unprotected and cold. Walking home through the park while those kids were still around could turn into a Grade A disaster. Drat that girl Patty. I swear I'll hate girls till the day I die.

The man walked toward us and, sounding grumpy, he said, "If I have to yank you off one by one, you'll be sorry, kids."

Instead of jumping down from the seat, Zoe called out, "Oh, Mr. Mike . . . Mike . . . Mr. Mike!"

He stopped and looked, actually looked, at all of us. "You're Pop's little girl from the hot dog stand, aren't you?"

That's when I recognized the man, too. He's a coffee-and-doughnuts customer. Big talker that she is, Zoe must have learned his name.

"And Patty Aylward, Mr. Maloney. Bill's girl from Sheridan Avenue. Bill Aylward that works in the Water Department," Patty added quickly.

"Mr. Mike, we never had our turn yet, we just got on and I never been . . . 'n' such big swings I . . . ." Zoe's words tumbled out as fast as she could draw breath.

Mike Maloney looked us over. "You showin' these new kids the park, Patty? That's a nice, neighborly thing to do. I s'pose I could go check the tool shed before I lock up. Five minutes. That's all, 'cause I want to get home to my supper. I'll be walkin' out of here same as you."

Looking over at the others, he asked, "You all had a turn?" and as they reluctantly nodded yes, he ordered, "Beat it, then. I'm locking up all but this one swing."

"Pump," the Donald Duck voice said again. "Pump hard. Stand up and we can get better leverage. Turn sideways. Hold on to the poles, if you can't keep your balance."

What a bossy talker this kid was! He was right, though, about standing to get a higher swing. Smoothly, he shifted his weight back and forth from side to side like a sailor on a ship in a storm. As the swing creaked and groaned, moving faster and higher, he leaned over the side and put a hand up to shade his eyes. Looking out over the grass, he shouted, "Land ho. Land ahead."

Zoe laughed out loud, and even I smiled. All together, we had more like ten minutes before Mr. Maloney came back. Long enough for me to correct Patty Aylward, who kept calling me "Jack," and to learn that the other kid's name was Abe Zalkin. The two of them walked out with Zoe and me. To be on the safe side, we went out right behind Mike Maloney.

"Hey, Zach, how can you tell which is the dogwood tree?" asked Abe, waving a hand toward the shadowy trees all around us.

Even if it hadn't been getting dark, I knew it was hopeless. I had to say, "I don't know."

"By its bark, of course," he told me with a straight face.

Boy, I had walked right into that one. This kid was so smooth, if a mosquito lit on him it would slide right off.

"Aren't you glad you got me, Zach? Wasn't it a good thing I know Mr. Mike?" asked Zoe happily as we crossed the street to the little park that sits like an island dividing Washington and Central. Feeling uppity about it all, she refused to take my hand.

"I'm walking with Patty," Zoe announced.

"Only if she's crossing to Central, too," I answered, but my attention was split as I wrestled with some worrying questions.

Would Abe and Patty walk us home? Did they live near us? Should I say anything about seeing them another day?

Abe, nodding toward the statue of a soldier carrying a gun, said, "Can you stay out? We usually pick up a game here."

I saw a bunch of kids sprawled on the steps around the base of the statue. Hope made my heart hop raggedly for a couple of beats.

"Well, I got Zoe to watch," I said cautiously.

"Nobody cares," said Patty. "Everybody has to watch somebody sometime or other."

It was that simple.

Because of their nicknames, it was easy to keep

straight who was who. "Tiny" Carlson was of course the tallest, and Louis "the Lip" Romano never said two words if one would do the trick.

When Abe Zalkin waved his hand at Tom Thomas to introduce him, Thomas interrupted, saying, "I already know him. He's Greek like me."

I couldn't tell much about these kids and their brainpower from looking at them, so I did a little testing. I said, "Drumhead and his ma stopped today at our store."

I waited and watched their puzzled faces. Just as I thought. Abe Zalkin got it first. He snickered while the others continued to look blank. Taking pity on them, he hunkered down and, spreading his legs as if he held a drum between his knees, he started pounding on his invisible drum. "Tom-tom. Tom Thomas. Don't you get it? This kid isn't such an apple-knocker, after all."

Apple-knocker must be another way of saying "hick" or "country bumpkin." Before I could think up an answer to that, the game started.

Hide 'n' Seek is played pretty much the same in Albany as in Cohoes, New York. And probably in Honolulu, too, now that I think about it. That Patty was fast for a girl, and once Zoe, who's small enough to lie down in the grass on the Central Avenue sloping side of the park and be invisible, brought everybody in free.

When they talked about the race planned for the

next day, I felt like an outsider again. Everybody had wagons or a partner to ride with. I couldn't tell if I was supposed to join them.

"It has to be later," Tom "Drumhead" Thomas insisted. "Tomorrow's a big holy day for us and I gotta go to church in the morning."

"Then you gotta go, too," said Abe, looking at me.

I didn't know what to say. In Cohoes, Mama didn't take time to go over to Troy church on holidays that came in the middle of the week. But in Albany it was just a short walk to St. Sophia's. Besides, Abe wasn't asking a question, he was making a statement.

"Okay. Go to church," he said in that bossy way of his. "Have lunch. We meet two o'clock, after Tiny's piano lesson. By the Armory."

Being Greek here in Albany was going to be a little easier than in Cohoes, I could see. With more of us around, I wouldn't have to keep explaining things, like how church always lasts at least three hours every time we go.

Abe continued, "The Lip has to bring his uncle Sal's stopwatch."

"Maybe," said Louie the Lip. "It's his, so . . ." and he shrugged.

"Zach, you don't have a . . ." and as I shook my head no, Abe switched and said, "Bring chalk, then."

141

I never have liked being ordered around like some little kid. Not in Cohoes, not in any city. If that Abe didn't understand that I was just as smart as he was, I could do without his company.

I stood up and, jumping down from the top step, said, "I'll be there tomorrow . . . maybe. You'll know I'm coming when you see me. C'mon, Zoe, you're going to turn into a pumpkin if you don't get home in two minutes."

He caught up with us just before we turned in the doorway of Number 7.

"Hey, what did I say that got your goat?"

"It's not *what* you said, it's *how* you said it. You sound like some general giving orders to the troops. To his very stupid troops. As if nobody else can think," I told him bluntly.

"It must come out sounding wrong because I don't always think in English, even though I can speak it pretty well now," he offered.

I was more confused after his explanation than before. What did he think *in,* if not English?

"Listen, I can tell you're not stupid. Don't think that. Take her upstairs. Come down again so we can finish."

By the time he said, "Don't think that," I couldn't help myself. I burst out laughing. It was plain that Abe Zalkin thought in capital letters and commands. He couldn't put together two sentences without making one of them an order. But he wasn't stupid, either, and he heard what he'd said. He grinned. It was as if the sun *and* the moon had both come out and lit up his face.

Abe tried again. "I mean, *please,* Mr. Zachary Poulos, would you like to come down to talk?"

When I ran back down the two flights of stairs after turning Zoe over to Mama, he was sitting on our bottom step, waiting. I was relieved to be rid of Zoe, as always, and I said so out loud.

"Your sister is a cute kid. I used to have a sister. An older one."

"What happened? You don't have one anymore?" I probably shouldn't have asked, but I was so startled the question popped out.

"She died in Cuba. Of pneumonia. She got sick on the ship going there. They didn't have any medicine on the ship."

"Is that where you're from? Cuba? Are you Spanish?"

"No. I'm Jewish. I was born in Austria, but we left when I was eight. We had to go to Cuba first and wait a year there to get in the U.S. I've been here just two years."

In the dark I could see only the whites of his eyes clearly, and I hoped he couldn't see the shock on my face. I'd read about refugees having to leave their own country and losing everything, but

I never thought to meet one in my own neighborhood.

Abe talked and I listened. He knows more about the war in Europe than anybody I've met, more even than grownups.

"Sometime, I'll show you my map of the world," he promised. "I use red pins for the British forces, black for the Germans. I move them every day, depending on where the battles are."

The window overhead screeched, and Mama's voice, which was only a little softer, floated down. "*Zaharia,* we have church tomorrow early. You must get ready tonight."

I grimaced. Drumhead had been right. And "getting ready" meant having to take an extra bath this week.

Abe got up quickly, and with that lit-up-all-over grin, he said, "See you tomorrow." This time it didn't sound like an order to me. Starting down the street, Abe tossed a good crack over his shoulder, "Well, as the chimp said when he slid down the giraffe's neck: So long."

Church took up the morning but not my mind. In between crossing myself and bowing my head, I was very busy hunting in my memory for riddles and knock-knock jokes to use on Abe. Rubbing up against somebody like him really exercises and polishes your brain.

As soon as church was over, Tom Thomas made a beeline for me outside. I debated trying some of my jokes on him.

"You want to go underground?" he asked mysteriously.

"Huh? Underground where?"

"You ever walked underground through the middle of a city? You scared of tunnels?" he asked, still not explaining. "If you're not, tell your ma that you're going home with me, and I'll show you a way to disappear from sight."

I hate to admit it, but he made me a little nervous with his talk about disappearing. Pictures of slimy rock caves and crawly sewer pipes came into my head. But how could I back off? Mama said yes, I could walk with him, so I had no choice in the end.

To my surprise, he turned up State Street and headed for the side door into the State Capitol Building. It seems you can walk in there even if you don't have any official business. We turned left down a hall lined with offices and then right, passing by big stone arches of what he called the Million Dollar Staircase. Finally, we stepped into a revolving door.

As we came out into a long, windowless corridor that sloped up, Thomas said, "This is it. You're in a tunnel under Capitol Park." He eyed me, asking hopefully, "You get the feeling that the walls are going to collapse? That the ceiling is going to come down on you?"

Boy, was I glad that I hadn't let him spook me out. I snorted. "You're kidding." Looking at him carefully, I said, "You're *not* kidding."

"Well, Dino Petrides gets sick when he stands in here," he said defensively. "And he can never walk to the end."

"He must have claustrophobia," I informed Drumhead, who looked goggle-eyed at the long word. "It's a fear of closed-in places, a sickness, really, so you can't call him chicken." Then, because I thought he should know, I added, "It's a Greek word, dummy."

Walking through the tunnel was pretty tame, actually, although I did get a kick out of knowing that people were walking around up above us on grass and sidewalks. We climbed two flights of steep stairs at the end and came out into the main floor of the State Office Building, which is Albany's skyscraper. Two short blocks after that, I was home.

That's where I got the *real* scare. Opening the back door, I saw Mama, sitting at the kitchen table. She had her head buried face down in her arms on the tabletop.

"Mama?" The thumping of my own pulse sounded louder to me than the word, which came out in a whisper. I tried again. "*Manoula?*" It's been years since I've called her "Mommy," but it just came out that way. If only she'd move . . . if only I could see her face . . . .

But when I saw her lift her head finally, it didn't make me feel better. Tears were streaming down her face, which somehow seemed all sharp bones at this moment. Mama never cries. Never.

"*Zaharia,* I . . . there were children, like you and *Zoeitsa* . . . ." She stopped, swallowed hard and stretched out her hands to me. "*Zaharia,* on the news, a submarine in Tinos Harbor . . . . Two torpedoes hit the quay. Tinos has the miraculous icon, so pilgrims—thousands and thousands—were there for the procession."

"But . . . but Greece isn't at war with anybody. I mean, nobody declared war." I stared at her, trying to make sense of what she had said.

"It's war. Undeclared, but war, nonetheless. Every day the Italians are sending battalions to Albania, so the king has ordered Greek troops to guard the northern frontiers," she said. "Your *Yiayia,* my mother . . . my brother—all there, and I'm here so far away from them at this awful time. Everybody I love . . . ." Her shoulders shook as she sobbed harder.

Maybe I ought to go away?

It's a terrible thing to see a grownup so helpless. My mother needed comforting, but I was the only one here. Trying to see straight when you're standing on your head is hard, and that's the way I felt: upside down.

Words. I'm supposed to be good with words. Help me now, God, to find some. Not a lot of words but the right ones.

Hesitantly, I put an arm around her shoulders and gave her a couple of little pats. "Mama, remember, three of us are right here. Papa, Zoe and me. You love us, don't you? And we're all together."

The only sign that she heard was a small squeeze she gave my hand.

Some of what Abe talked about last night came back to me. "Us being here in America is better, because we can really help them there. If war does come, they can't work but we can. We can still be working here and send money—maybe even tickets for them to come over—or maybe medicines and stuff by the Red Cross."

Mama's big, dark eyes full of tears looked up and focused finally on my face. (I'd never noticed before how much alike she and Zoe look.) I gave it one more try. "Anyway, Greece will win. Some general with a sword will come out like Alexander the Great and lead them to victory."

Mama didn't actually smile, but her face looked as if the muscles had loosened up a little. She stopped crying and said, "Somehow I don't think this is a war for swords, *Zaharia,* but you are right. We have one another. What we must do is work hard . . . and pray."

Like an old lady, she pulled herself up slowly from the chair, and for one very long second she rested her hand on top of my head. She had to reach up to do it because she's a short lady and we're just about eye to eye now.

"What have you been doing behind my back, *Zaharia?*"

My heart jumped—out of habit, I guess, because I don't really have anything on my conscience just now. It turned out that she was talking about how I'd grown this summer. Before I changed my Sunday pants, she measured how much to let down the cuffs, and she had me try on a whole pile of shirts to make sure I had some good ones for school.

It was so much better than having her cry that I didn't complain about being held up. In fact, I stuck around a little longer to make sure she had truly stopped crying, before going to the store for lunch with Zoe.

On our way to meet the kids on Lark Street hill, I warned Zoe, "Don't beg for a ride in anybody's wagon, or for a turn in the race." I added that if they said she had to go home, she'd have to go. I couldn't take any risks yet with these new connections.

The Armory sidewalk is smoother and longer,

so that's where they decided to race. Going off the curb or across the curb would put you out of the race. Winner would be whoever turned the corner at Elk Street first. Only the best drivers could manage that without slowing down or braking, so it was a true and good test. Patty Aylward suggested we do heats like the soapbox derby because there were nine kids and only four wagons: one metal Red Flyer, two big wooden ones and a little homemade one.

"No girl drives *my* wagon," Louie the Lip declared.

"This one can ride in mine," said Tiny Carlson, plopping Zoe into his. "We're going down together. She can add weight, and I'll bet I go faster."

"I think she'll slow you down," Abe argued.

The argument was just warming up when the scream came. I wished with all my might that I was not hearing what I thought I heard. No use. It was Zoe shrieking "Help! Stop me!" Hanging on to the wagon tongue, she was shooting down the hill and picking up speed every second.

"Stop . . . Turn . . . Turn your . . . Put your . . . ." Shouting, bumping into and tripping over one another, everybody was trying to work out what to do next.

But Elk Street was coming up fast. Zoe'd never get herself steered around the corner, and the light was green for cars from that direction.

I launched myself down the hill. From the corner of my eye, I saw blurs moving on either side of me. The blur on my right pulled ahead. Taking my eyes off Zoe for a split second, I saw that it was Patty Aylward. Abe Zalkin was about even with me but on the other, far side of the wagon. I put on a burst of speed.

Patty might reach Zoe first. But was she strong enough to brake the speeding wagon to a halt? Patty had pulled even with the wagon now, but instead of veering to it, she kept straight on. What the heck was she doing?

Then, forgetting her, I got ready to jump on. I landed in the wagon at the same time as Abe Zalkin from the other side. *Cr-rack!* Tears sprang into my eyes as our heads banged together. I put my foot down to brake and Abe did likewise on his side. But our momentum carried us off the curb.

Ahead I saw Patty. Standing smack in the middle of the street, she was waving the oncoming cars to a halt. (That's the exact moment that I stopped hating girls.) We hit the opposite curb with a bone-shaking thump that bounced our front wheels up over, and at last, we halted.

"Phew!" said Abe, moving his head gently as if to see if it were still fastened.

Yours truly, Zachary Athanasius Poulos, famous for talking, had nothing to say.

Patty, collapsing on the curb next to us, complained breathlessly, "Louie should've brought the stopwatch. I bet we set a new world record for sprints."

In a shaky voice Zoe said, "I knew I'd be okay. I knew Zach could ZAP the wagon."

Abe raised his eyebrow, questioningly, and Patty's blue flame eyes widened as I explained, "It's sort of a joke. Because both our initials are Z.A.P., we kid around about having magical powers."

A startled look spread over Patty's face, and I added hastily, "We don't actually bel—"

"Do you know what my middle name is?" Patty demanded, interrupting me. "I don't usually tell anybody. It's Zelda. Don't you see? I have the same initials, only mine go P.Z.A."

"You'll never believe this," said Abe, slapping his leg. He winced and said, "I am on my passport Abram Pincus Zalkin. A.P.Z."

"What's so funny, you guys?" Zoe asked over and over, as the three of us laughed like lunatics.

"What do you suppose the odds are against finding a combination like us? Probably a billion to one," Abe said finally, after he'd wiped the tears of laughter.

"Attention: announcing a special club," I said, "as of this fifteenth day of August 1940, for those lucky people with the initials Z.A.P. or any variation thereof. It shall be known as The Three Musketeers."

"What's a Musket Ear?" asked Zoe.

"Musketeers rescue people in distress, like you, Zoe," I said. "They swear to help one another even if it kills them. And to be in our Musketeer Club, you have to have our combination of initials, Z.A.P."

"Then it's four, Zach, not three. You can't count. My 'nitials are Z.A.P. and I wanna be a Musket Ear, too."

That's how come Zoe put her hand on, too, when we piled our hands one on top of the other and made the pact: one for all and all for one.